You're not alone . . .

When the man of your life leaves you for another woman . . . the world as you knew it comes crashing down. I know. I've been there.

I thought at first that maybe it really was possible to die of a broken heart. I learned that it takes a long time to recover and that even when you think you're over it, some days you're suddenly back at square one. I found out that support is crucial and that it sometimes comes from unlikely sources.

And I determined from the outset never to pretend that what had happened had not *really* happened. . . .

Perhaps partly due to that attitude, women in the same boat wanted to talk to me. I started to make notes on my experiences and theirs—and I was amazed. . . .

What I discovered . . . is that my own survival-recovery experiences dovetailed with those of the women I talked to. It's not just how he acts but *what you go through* that follows a pattern. You need to know what to do to get from here to there, how to work your way beyond betrayal into new strength.

Stick with me. In *Dumped!* I'll tell you what I had to learn the hard way—and what a lot of the dumpees I have met are still trying to work their way through.

DUMPED!

A Survival Guide for
the Woman Who's Been Left
by the Man She Loved

Sally Warren
with Andrea Thompson

HarperPaperbacks
A Division of HarperCollins*Publishers*

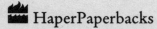

HaperPaperbacks

A Division of HarperCollins*Publishers*
10 East 53rd Street, New Yrok, N.Y. 10022-5299

A hardcover edition of this book was published in 1998 by
Cliff Street Books, an imprint of HarperCollins Publishers.

ISBN 0-06-109772-1

HarperCollins®, ▦®, and HarperPaperbacks™
are trademarks of HarperCollins Publishers, Inc.

First HarperPaperbacks printing: March 1999

Printed in the United States of America

Visit HarperPaperbacks on the World Wide Web at
http://www.harpercollins.com

❖ 10 9 8 7 6 5 4 3 2 1

To Brenda Kinsella,
who came out of nowhere to be there,
for Ginny and John Richards,
who cushioned the blow, and
for my oldest friend, Barbara Gillam,
who has always been on my side

Contents

Preface

When the man of your life leaves you for another woman, when he who once loved you desperately now doesn't want to look you in the eye, the world as you knew it comes crashing down. I know. I've been there.

I thought at first that maybe it really was possible to die of a broken heart. I learned that it takes a long time to recover and that even when you think you're over it, some days you're suddenly back at square one. I found out that support is crucial and that it sometimes comes from unlikely sources.

And I determined from the outset never to pretend that what had happened had not *really* happened (as in "Well, we both decided separation was a good idea right now" or "Things didn't work out" or other evasions). I saw that when I put a name (dumped!) to my situation, people felt less uncomfortable around me.

Perhaps partly due to that attitude, women in the same boat wanted to talk to me. As the idea for this book grew in my mind, I started to make notes on my experiences and theirs—and I was amazed. By and large our stories were the same. While the details certainly differed, the big realities surfaced again and again.

It begins with the dumper's behavior. For example, after a period of some months or even years of his not quite *being there*, he tells you he's moving on. Even if you suspected trouble, you're invariably staggered by this announcement.

And then the dumper tends to choose an inappropriate, perhaps even ghastly time to announce his departure. You may be coping with a sick mother or about to get terminated at work, maybe Christmas or your anniversary or birthday is next week—nothing holds a man back when he decides to go.

He almost always has a new woman lined up; you're dumped *for* somebody else. A woman will leave a relationship because it's bad in many ways and she has come to the conclusion over time that it's not fixable. And usually she "gives notice." On the other hand, most men who leave do so because they're involved with someone new. Very rarely does a man go from something to nothing.

What I discovered—and here is the raison d'être for *Dumped!*—is that my own survival/recovery experiences dovetailed with those of the women I talked to. It's not just how he acts but *what you go through* that follows a pattern. You need to know what to do to get from here to there, to work your way beyond betrayal into new strength.

Stick with me. In *Dumped!* I'll tell you what I had to learn the hard way—and what a lot of the dumpees I have met are still struggling to figure out:

- How to see it coming. Heed these warning signals, and you won't get dumped again!
- How to survive the initial shock, when you feel you've been blindsided by a large wooden mallet.
- How to get through the bleeding and wallowing stage. While you will *need* some time to wallow, you can keep yourself from drowning in the misery of it all.
- How your dumper will act, in the beginning and over time. If you know that, you can avoid costly and/or humiliating mistakes as you forge your separation from him.
- How other people may talk to you—*handle* you—in ways that will make you want to either smash them over the head or burst into tears.
- What to say to make others view you as a class act and not a bitter bitch.
- How to recognize if you are secretly waiting for him to "get over it" and come back to you—and thus postponing your forward progress.
- What to do about men—your ex's friends or business associates, old boyfriends, other women's husbands who are eager to offer solace, or the new man who looks tempting.
- How to have some laughs about it all—finally—because getting dumped is surely one of life's major bad jokes.

To be dumped resonates with a meaning all its own.

To be dumped is not quite the same as:

- Splitting up
- Seeing less of each other
- Deciding mutually to call it quits

To be dumped presupposes that:

- You loved him, he loved you.
- You were partners in an intimate, committed relationship, sexually, emotionally, psychologically.
- You were an acknowledged couple, by family and friends.
- He ended all that, in a way that was hurtful, fairly unexpected, and absolutely unequivocal.

This is a book of specific suggestions on how to navigate the uncharted seas you have so rudely been cast upon. It's based on the experiences of over one hundred women who were unceremoniously left by the men with whom they expected to walk off into the sunset.

They range in age from twenty-four to fifty-eight at the time of their dumping. Some had been married at the time of the split for between five and thirty-eight years. Others were unmarried but in committed relationships of three to fourteen years' duration. They talk here at length about their lives before, during, and after the great dump.

Listen to what they learned, and then plan your own road map out of the pain of betrayal and into your new life.

You *will* survive and you *can* move on. If you play your cards right, you will be smarter, stronger, and maybe even happier than you were before you got *dumped!*

Acknowledgments

This book has benefited immeasurably from the contributions of many terrific women who were willing to share the experience of being dumped. Each one wanted to help others through the rough waters that every dumpee is forced to navigate. I am grateful to all of them for being so wonderfully giving and candid.

Andrea and I extend our thanks to our editor, Diane Reverand, for believing in this book (and sticking with the title) and to our literary agents, Stedman Mays and the late Connie Clausen, for their encouragement and enthusiasm. Our appreciation also to Meaghan Dowling, who was on duty in the formative stages of this enterprise.

A special thanks to Andrée Abecassis, a friend of long standing, who encouraged us in this project.

Lastly, I would like to thank four Warrens-by-blood for keeping the lines of communication open: my three stepchildren, Catherine, Bruce, and Patrick, and my brother-in-law Terry. And, of course, a salute to FMPW, without whom there would be no book.

—SW

Introduction

Beginnings of the End: How a Man Dumps You, and the First Thing You Need to Know to Survive

We might more accurately call this an epilogue followed by an introduction.

First, you get the news that the man you love is leaving you and thus bringing your joint life to an end. All at once, ready or not, you're introduced to your new life, one you can only dimly perceive.

Perhaps, like Lynn, you got the news over the phone. "Eric called me from a business trip," she says, "and told me he would not be coming home for Christmas the following week. I got this call just before I went to an important business luncheon, and I still don't know how I made it through without sobbing.

"I knew he'd had an affair once, years back. We saw a therapist over that. I never dreamed he would fall in love with someone else, or leave me. I still believed—and he kept telling me—that we'd work it all out. Until that phone call."

Christmas or a birthday or some other festive, romantic, or significant occasion seems to loom large in many dumper/dumpee scenarios. Marianne and her boyfriend of five years had arranged a Valentine's Day getaway weekend in a charming country inn. "That Saturday morning we went out for breakfast with some friends," she remembers, "and Kent seemed quiet. We got home, started getting ready to go off on our little holiday. Kent was still acting quiet, and then he turned to me and said, 'I don't know if I love you anymore.' A couple of months later I found out he had left me for a woman he had met six weeks earlier at a tanning place. After five years I was dumped for a nineteen-year-old tanning salon queen."

Maybe your dumper conveyed the news in a neutral corner. Emily and Jim had lived together for three years, during the last four months of which he was spending most evenings at work, at the gym, "with the guys," anywhere, it seemed, but in their apartment with her. "I was just getting in from work on this Wednesday, about six, and the phone was ringing," Emily says. "It was Jim. He said he was going to stop in Woody's, this neighborhood place we liked, and why didn't I meet him there for a beer. I was thrilled—this was the kind of thing he hardly ever suggested anymore. I got there, we talked about general stuff. Then he said, 'I don't know how to tell you this, so I'll just say it. I met somebody else.'"

Maybe other people heard the news at the same time you did. Gretchen learned she was being dumped when her husband of thirty-four years made a public announcement of the fact: "Keith had just been awarded an honorary degree. We were at a celebratory party afterward with about three hundred people, many from his firm. Keith made a little speech, at the end of which he said, 'I think you all also should know that Gretchen's and my marriage is over, at my volition.'

"Later I learned he had been having an affair with his assistant. He told me that she had a spot on her cervix and she might be dead within a year. He wanted to marry her because they had to have their happiness, and they were in love from the time they met, which was approximately ten years earlier. They did get married, five years ago, and she's not dead yet."

Your dumper may have acted upset and agitated, as did Joanne's: "It was a Sunday night. I'd just gotten back from picking up our daughter at her summer camp and got the two kids into bed. My husband said he had to tell me something, and he was extremely emotional, almost teary. He said he was having an affair, it had been going on for a while. All this was total news to me. He's since married this woman. She was a friend of mine."

Or he may have been unusually calm, even matter-of-fact. Janet remembers coming home early from a business meeting, walking into her living room, and seeing her partner and a woman from his office sitting on the couch drinking wine: "It was a scene from a Henry James novel—something went *click!* in my mind. Everything looked on the up-and-up, but there was something about their posture, the look on their faces, not to mention drinking some damned good white burgundy on a Saturday afternoon. Then I had a moment of feeling, I'm going to be sick.

"I said nothing to him that evening, and he said nothing to me. It was just business as usual. The next day I was watching him playing with the dog and said, sort of lightly, 'That dog gets more attention from you than I do.' And he said, also sort of lightly, 'Well, maybe we should split.'"

Perhaps the news came just when you thought you and he were over a bad patch and all was fine again. Leslie's husband had been working later and later, acting evasive, and looking guilty, she says: "I believe he wanted me to find out, and one morning I just put it to him and said what the hell was going on? He admitted he was having an affair, and I insisted that he put an end to it.

"He told me he would and then later told me he had. And I thought it would be a good idea to get away for a while, so we went off for a trip to Italy. We had a fabulous, loving, romantic time, just the two of us. He came back all excited, telling everybody what a swell trip it had been. One week later, he told me he was leaving me for this woman."

Chances are, whether you were married or in your relationship for three years or thirty, knew he was playing around or drifting away or not, suspected something was troubling him or sailed ahead in the belief that all was well, you were dumped pretty much the way Lynn, Emily, and the rest were:

- Your man announced one day that your relationship was over.

And D-Day remains forever etched in your memory—the date, the time, the place, the food you ate, the clothes you wore. The explanation, such as it was, may have been that he wasn't sure he wanted to be married anymore, that he wasn't ready to *get* married, that he didn't think you two were right for each other, that he was in love with someone else, that there absolutely *wasn't* someone else but he just had to have space, that you both had changed and there was no sense in continuing, or any variation of the above.

- Two points were absolutely clear: he wanted out, and he was presenting you with an emotional fait accompli. He would not discuss it, you had no say, the relationship was simply over.

Says one dumpee: "You can't sit down together, two equals with one problem, and try to work it out. No matter how each of you was acting before, whatever was going wrong, the bottom line is that when he decides to walk, you have no choices left."

Says a married dumpee: "If your husband doesn't want to be married, you cease being married, regardless of what you want or the law says."

- You were dumbfounded.

You had no idea this was coming. Even if ripples or tidal waves or discontent had defined your joint life of late, you never thought it would come to this.

Somewhere down the road—after you've emerged from your running-on-automatic-pilot-dealing-with-the-pain-and-anger haze—you'll look back, and you may very likely wonder, as one woman says, "How could I have been so stupid? How could I not have known?"

You'll look back and see the signs. Let's take a look at what those signs might have been.

21 Sure Signs You Are About to Be Dumped

Our aim is not to stir up painful memories or lead you to reflect on what a jerk you were, but on the road to getting over being dumped, it's useful to acknowledge where you've been and how it all played out.

And if that new life you're heading toward includes a new man, wiser though you will be, it's still an excellent idea to review this little primer of the signs and signals of a man who is working up to leaving you. Here are the typical scenarios of betrayal in the works. Forewarned is forearmed. You will *not* be caught in the dark again.

1) Walking down the street, he tends to stride a few steps ahead of you.

Says one dumpee: "I was always feeling like the little concubine, trailing behind and chugging along to catch up to him." Try to take his hand, and he suddenly becomes fascinated by the shop windows you're passing and moves away from you to look in them. He's acting sort of muted these days about being touched.

2) He calls you a lot.

He phones from his office to say he has a late meeting and doesn't know when it will be breaking up, or from his hotel when he's on a business trip to say he's arrived but the hotel isn't comfortable so his group may be moving to another one.

In fact, during the early stages of being dumped, you're getting daytime calls from him all the time, more than ever before. Later you realize he was calling you so you wouldn't call him. Ask him where he will be when, and he can't say exactly.

3) Or he doesn't call you at all.

Where once he checked in with you routinely during the day, now you don't hear from him.

One woman's lawyer husband started arriving home from work at one or two in the morning. "It wasn't like him not to phone," she says, "but I wouldn't hear anything and never knew when to expect him. Once, very late, I actually ran down to his office—I didn't have the number for building security—to look for him because I was convinced he must have collapsed or something. Now I know he was off with this woman."

4) He's working late a lot.

He leaves messages on your answering machine many an afternoon to say he won't be able to make it for dinner. When you're together, he goes off abruptly for evening or weekend meetings that he hadn't mentioned earlier.

Says one woman: "Bob was in real estate, and during the last months before he left he was always working late. I can look back now and say, 'Well, wasn't I a dope!' You don't show property at night. But at the time, the furthest thing from my mind was another woman because he had never been a man like that. So if I thought anything at all, it might have been that everybody's working long hours these days."

5) His explanations of where he is and what he's doing become more imaginative and outlandish as time passes.

"I was on the Madison Avenue bus heading home," he says, "but I jumped off to save fourteen Boy Scouts, and then I ended up taking them all to dinner." In retrospect, he seemed almost to be pushing you to find him out.

6) **When you do spend time together, he wants other people around, preferably not other couples.**

Suggest going out for Sunday brunch, and he says, "I'll call up Frank and Max and Bill and Polly and see if they want to meet us." He appears happiest when you're both at a large, crowded, noisy event or place where he doesn't have to talk to you too much.

7) **He picks fights.**

He's often irritable or vaguely annoyed. He provokes you into starting a spat. There's a lot of unreasonable anger coming out of nowhere.

Says one dumpee: "I recognized that he was not happy because he was angry all the time, largely at me. I kept putting it down to his imminent retirement—this man was a confirmed workaholic. I thought that once he got through the idea of retirement and into it, all of this would settle down. As it turned out, that wasn't the problem."

8) **Intimate conversation wanes.**

When you're together, the talk is not as personal, confidential, or easily familiar as before. Where he used to describe an argument he just had with somebody at work or why he's worried about his kid sister, now he sticks to telling you a joke he heard or what's wrong with the Yankee bullpen. He's bringing you in on his daily life as little as possible. At home he turns on the TV as soon as he gets in.

9) **Emotionally, he's not there for you.**

He has a strangely flat reaction to *your* overtures, gestures, gossipy stories, plans for a party. He's usually looking somewhere over your shoulder when you're telling him any of this. Or he suddenly comes to and says, "Yeah, OK, get to the point." This in itself, says one woman, tends to throw cold water on your efforts to have an intimate conversation: "You begin to edit everything you say, or you start feeling you must be light and amusing all the time. It seemed there was never anything important enough to say to this guy that would make him stop and listen. He was tuned out."

You mention that you think you're getting a cold or that you should be hearing on Tuesday if you'll be moved up to zone manager in your department. Later he doesn't ask how you're feeling or whether the promotion came through. He's forgotten.

He doesn't laugh at your jokes, which causes you to laugh excessively in compensation, which causes you to feel like an idiot.

At family gatherings, he's likely to be quiet and distant, not really getting into things with the others. Little amusing or sentimental incidents of a family nature don't register with him.

Says Emma: "We were driving somewhere with the kids, and suddenly something reminded Susie and Becky of a stuffed carrot that we bought on another trip a year earlier. This carrot was so unbelievably ridiculous and ugly that we decided we had to have it. The girls and I started talking about the stupid carrot and laughing, and Bill was just sitting there. He didn't remember the carrot incident at all."

10) Sex has petered out.

He's seldom in the mood. He's tired (all those late nights at work). He may be getting it elsewhere.

Says Laura: "Oh yes, sex became less frequent, no doubt as his frequency with his new girlfriend increased. If I initiated anything, he'd turn me away. And let's face it, rare is the guy who turns it down from anyone. The light still didn't dawn."

Another woman says lovemaking went out the window: "We didn't have sex for three months, which was a huge deal because it had always been a couple of times a week. I had little desire for it because I sensed something was going on. I said to him, 'Tell me what's happening. I'm a really open person. Just say it, and I'll feel better and you'll feel better and maybe we'll make passionate love!' I was talking to a brick wall."

On the other hand, he may have no trouble at all with straight sex in the dark. He's let the pre-

and post-intercourse activities fall by the wayside, however.

11) Or sex is hotter and heavier than ever.

He's suddenly keen for more, perhaps in new positions and places other than your bed. This is not necessarily a sign of passion. If it's true, as some commentators have observed, that couples have the most sex the year after marriage and the year before divorce, his behavior now may signal a dumping in the works.

Angela says that for two or three months before her husband dumped her, they went from routine sex to fantastic sex: "I have two theories about this. He knew he was going to walk, and he felt guilty and was trying to make it up to me. Or his mistress had gotten his hormones churning again."

12) He says he needs space.

He's removing himself from the scene in small ways, such as suddenly going out for a walk in the middle of a dinner party, or telling you to go on ahead to the beach place you're renting with friends and he'll join you a couple of days later than planned. There's a definite separating of interests, yours and his; suddenly he's into a lot of pickup basketball with the guys.

After he's made a few of these escapes, you ask him why he always seems to be heading out the door, and he replies, "I just need some space. Just cut me some slack. It has nothing to do with you and me."

Says one dumpee: "A friend told me the other day her boyfriend had made this very remark to her, and I said, 'Let me translate that for you: there is another woman.' I didn't want to be the one to hurt her, but for a year and a half after my husband walked out on me after a ten-year marriage, I continued to believe he was just needing his space."

13) He finds you lacking.

Not loving you anymore translates into not loving the little things you do, the little ways you are.

When Mark, Annie's boyfriend of seven years and a fellow musician, was getting ready to dump her, he suddenly found her tastes and behavior too unconventional for his liking: "One day Mark said, 'You know, you and I don't have that much in common. I'm pretty traditional—you're not.' I said, 'Mark, you're a rock musician. You go on the road. What's so traditional? I don't go on the road. We live together, it's an exclusive relationship as far as I'm concerned. That's pretty traditional. But who are you seeing who's more traditional than me?' He insisted there was no one else. But it was obvious to me that I wasn't meeting some standard he was admiring in another woman, who turned out to be this twenty-three-year-old chick with an agenda—marriage and kids."

Greta's husband, before he walked, suddenly didn't like the way she dressed, the way she fed the children. Greta says: "The way men are able to do this to you is they demonize you. They have to make you into the bad guy so they have an excuse to treat you this way. Suddenly you're not this, you're not that, you're too this, you're too that—no matter what it is. They have to justify it, otherwise *they're* the bad guy."

You're spending an evening with friends, and he makes a little crack at your expense—"That's Marcy for you, nothing if not literal-minded." He's starting, consciously or not, to manifest to others his discontent with you.

14) He changes.

He's developed new passions, for sports, music, food, or hobbies he had no interest in before.

Rachel's husband, during the waning days of their marriage, acted in ways many dumpees have observed in their men: "Sam left just after his thirtieth birthday. For about half a year before that, he was taking Italian lessons, saxophone lessons, he started running. He talked about buying a new car. As it turned out, he was seeing someone who was twenty years old, and clearly he needed to be feeling on top of his game."

Says another dumpee: "My husband was fifty-six. He started biking—alone, I thought—and going to a personal trainer twice a week. This was a man whose previous favorite activity was watching football on TV."

He's spiffing himself up, looking good. If you have usually been involved in the purchase of his clothes, you now notice new items you had nothing to do with. Your man, never that interested in his wardrobe before, suddenly starts sporting distinctively striped shirts and unusual ties.

15) He evades all talk of the future.

Mention something about "in the fall" or "after Katie leaves for camp," and he doesn't seem to hear you. Any reference on your part to future plans or events fails to engage his attention.

He doesn't even want to talk about next Saturday. Where once he liked lining up or at least suggesting plans for a weekend or two to come, now he's vague. You don't hear from him anymore the words *we* and *our*, as in "We should do that Alpine hike again before it gets too hot out." He doesn't refer to "our place"; he calls it "the apartment" or "the house."

16) There are a lot of wrong numbers ringing at your home.

You pick up the phone and it goes dead. Or he picks up the phone and says in a hushed voice, "Sorry, you must have the wrong number."

17) He encourages your private pursuits.

Tell him you're thinking of taking a tour of France with your sister, starting graduate school, or applying for a job in another city, and he says, "Great! Go for it." He wants you to start feeling as separate from him as he is feeling from you.

18) He says he's got to go to Dallas on business for a week. Later you see him looking for his passport.

He's actually off to Acapulco for romance, not with you.

19) You and he have always shared thoughts, maybe even a little inside joke, about a mutual friend or acquaintance. Now he avoids all mention of her.

Or, a variation on the theme, she and he work in the same office, and he's always talked about her in positive terms. But at the holiday party you and he attend together, he seems to be going out of his way to steer clear of her. His other coworkers, some of whom you know, are acting strained around you and don't spend much time talking to you as a couple.

She's the new woman in his life.

20) When you ask him what's wrong, he doesn't want to talk about it.

You *have* been picking up clues, you think there's a problem, and you've come up with some possible answers—job stress or tight finances or trouble in bed. You say to him, "Let's talk about it."

Nothing's wrong, he says, he's just under a lot of pressure at work, it will be over soon, everything will be fine, don't bug him about it. Or yes, he says, he's got a lot on his mind, but it's nothing to do with you. Or he gets snappish: "No! Nothing's the matter! Why do you keep asking me?" Your repeated overtures to get things back on track go nowhere.

When Rachel's husband was suddenly signing up for lessons left and right and breaking the budget on new clothes, she knew something was afoot: "This was about two months before he left. I said to him, 'You seem to be really struggling with something. Is it anything to do with me?' He said, and I quote, 'This is just about me turning thirty. It's a little blip in our lifetime together. It has absolutely nothing to do with you or us.' And I believed him, so I left him alone. We all believe these guys! We are so *involved* in this thing."

Says Annie: "Mark and I started working together on the music for a children's play we had in mind. Every time we'd come to some sweet parts about home and family, he'd get emotional and go in the bathroom. It was clear to me that he was harboring tremendous guilt. I said, 'Look, Mark, what's happening here? I'm not a ball and chain. We've been together for a long time, we're friends. Why don't you just tell me what's going on?' He said, 'It's nothing, there's nobody, I hate myself.' Then he started going to a shrink."

21) A friend decides to clue you in.

Most likely if the people you socialize with spot your man with the new love interest, they won't tell you. Blowing the whistle on a cheating spouse or lover is dicey business, even for a good friend.

But it's possible that a friend may drop hints by asking you questions designed to open the way for a candid talk: "Is everything OK with you and George? No reason, I was just wondering." You don't particularly *want* to have a talk. You trust your man.

Erica and John were close friends with another couple, Joe and Pat. Says Erica: "One day Joe called me up—this is probably about three months before I got dumped—and suggested we have lunch. We were all good pals, and I said, 'Sure, let's have lunch.' We met and we're talking, and he's kind of circling around the issue of John—was I aware that John didn't seem very happy these days and so on. Everything was nebulous. I thought he was being nosy and critical, so, fool that I was, I essentially told him it was none of his business.

"That night I talked to John about it. I said, 'Joe has told me you're not yourself. What's the story? Is there something I can help with?' And he said it was just job pressures."

•   •   •

Maybe one or some of these signs and signals register in your consciousness, and you feel damn sure there's more to this than meets the eye. Of course you will work it out, you think, because the two of you together have been the center of everything.

Then one day he says:

I can't go on with this any longer.

I'm not happy.

I'm not coming home.

This isn't working. We're very different people.

I want out.

Guess what? You've been dumped.

And here's the first thing you need to know: getting over it will take time.

I know from my own experience—and from talking to Rachel, Annie, and the other women whose voices you will hear throughout this book— that the dumped woman has suffered a war wound. You're bruised and traumatized; you will not heal easily. In the beginning, you're moving on automatic pilot. Some days, that you are moving at all should be considered an accomplishment.

Joanna, married at age eighteen and dumped twenty-five years and three children later, says: "Indeed, the marriage had not been perfect, but I believed it was essentially a good one. And then he left me to marry someone else. The thing that both appalled and fascinated me was that after twenty-five years of living together, the door just closed. I mean it simply closed. The person I could share my most intimate thoughts with, the person I believed I could trust more than anyone else—this person was suddenly gone. I didn't know who to talk to. My children, my husband, they had been the broad parameters of my life. I simply didn't know what to do."

Emily, twenty-six, whose boyfriend took her out for a beer to tell her that he was involved with someone else, says: "Jim and I met in college, hung out together off and on. After we graduated, we both ended up in advertising jobs in New York, and we fell in love. We were together, inseparable really, for over three years. I knew his parents and brothers, he knew mine. Until the last few months, every way we talked, all the assumptions—on both our parts, I believed—had to do with us being together, for keeps.

"My mother says to me now, 'So you broke up, so what? You're young, you'll meet lots of other men' and so on. She doesn't get it. First of all, *we* didn't break up—he left me. Second, I wanted *him,* and he wanted me, and now he doesn't."

Getting through it takes time. And that's a reality to cling to because soon the people around you will be suggesting you snap out of it and get on with life. Progress often feels like one step forward and two back. You *will* get over it and get on with it but only when you're damn well ready.

There's no shortcut to coping with the betrayal you have sustained. If you try to put it behind you too quickly, either you will leave yourself open to being betrayed again because the wound hasn't healed, or you will run around encased in such thick armor you won't trust a man ever again.

One woman came to that realization slowly. Anita required emergency surgery just one month after her boyfriend of six years moved out and in with someone new. While she understood that physically she'd need a long period of recuperation, it wasn't until much later that she realized she was also in for a slow mental and emotional recovery: "For a full year or more I wasn't capable of feeling comfortable or even normal around a man, and I feared I never would. Then I began to see that I was trying to force myself to recover from Alan's betrayal. I knew that my body would heal in its own time—I had to let my emotional self heal the same way."

Know that it will take time.

Coping, the Early Stages

From Shock to Bleeding and on to Wallowing in the Pain

When the man you love has just left, you think it can't be happening. The first night you're in shock, which is actually helpful because you feel numb. Then later you wonder how you can live with so much pain. Your heart literally aches. Even if you had suspicions that all was not well, this is beyond bearing. This is the ultimate in rejection, the betrayal of your trust, the death of your future.

We call this period of early pain management the time of "walking wounded," and all the dumpees we've talked to know just what that means: you are unbelievably hurt, you are embarrassed, you are drained, and you don't see how you will survive. There will be days when you feel vaguely OK and days when you can't get out of bed in the morning. You will obsess. You will act irrationally. Often there's no rhyme or reason to what you do.

How long will you be walking wounded? The

acute phase, the I-don't-want-to-get-out-of-bed-ever-again part, according to the women we've talked to, can last for weeks or even months.

Says Lori: "I'd get up, go to my job—nobody at work knew anything was going on—and return directly home. I wouldn't answer the phone. Just ate some yogurt and went to bed. This went on for about three months."

Says Janet: "One thing about having kids, you have to keep going. I just kept saying 'I have to do this next, do that next.' For about six months I'd go to work, and there I must have been doing OK because when my supervisor learned later what had happened she said she would never have guessed.

"Every evening I'd cry all the way home in the car, get to the house, wipe away the tears, get the kids settled for the night, and then cry myself to sleep. I can't remember much about anything during that time."

After the worst of it is over, you'll still by no means be back to normal, maybe even for years.

Says Susan: "I would have to say I was almost a basket case for a good three years. I'd been married for nineteen years, so this was tough going. I was able to function just at a bare minimum."

Says Sarah: "A friend told me getting over it takes a year for every two years you were together. I remember being horrified because I was thinking I'd just spent six years with Peter. In fact, that turned out to be pretty much bang on."

But we're not going to brood anymore at this point about three-year scenarios and such. With

Dumped! as your guide, your path into your new life will be swifter and smoother than you might imagine.

Right now, how can you get through the first day, the first week, go to work, eat dinner, sleep, get up?

Here are the basics of early pain management.

20 Steps to Get through the Worst of It and Start Feeling Better

1) **Set up a support system.**

   This is number one. Find—at once!—within the first three days!—the person (or maybe it will be persons) who will *be there* for you, who will keep you from going off the deep end at four in the morning.

   She (or perhaps he) must, of course, have an interest in your welfare but, almost as important, must have the time to devote to it because being your primary support person is going to take a lot of hours and a lot of energy.

   You can call this marvelous person anytime (and you will); she calls you to see how you're feeling; she makes you go out to lunch or a movie; eventually she drags you to a party when you think you can't possibly face it.

   Your support person may emerge at once from among the group of people you call or who regularly call you (and as soon as the news that you've been dumped gets out, which is immediately, you'll be hearing from a lot of friends, enemies, and vaguely interested by-standers).

She may be your best friend. She may be your sister. She might be your mother, although in our experience mothers don't make ideal motivators. Whoever she is, she may be the one you'd least expect.

Says Molly: "One of the surprising things to me about this whole miserable time was that some friends I expected to really be there for me weren't too available. And one woman, the one who became my main support, kind of appeared out of nowhere. She had been a casual friend— someone Mike and I saw as part of a couple. I really didn't know her very well.

"She sensed, though, that I was in bad shape, and for weeks she was my literal lifeline. I should also say she was one of the busiest people I know. She'd call me several times a day to see how I was doing, let me call her in the middle of the night, take me out to lunch where I would sit and sob. This must have been a drag for her. But she was there for me. She was heaven sent."

If your primary support person—sister, best friend, casual acquaintance—does not appear, go and find her.

Think of all the people you know who might be candidates.

Call candidate number one. Don't be proud. Lay it all out on the table. Don't put her on the spot, but do tell her what's happened and what you're looking for; for example: "Louise, I'm really in rough shape. I know you as a friend and a kind person. It would mean a lot to me right now if I could count on you to be my main support—someone I can call in the middle of the night when I think I'm going crazy, someone to keep an eye on me. Is that OK? Can you do it? Do you have the time to give me?"

If this thoroughly scares Louise off, or if she weighs her own current life and responsibilities and tells you with regret that she cannot be what you need her to be, offer her your thanks, no hard feelings, and go on to candidate number two.

And then you must find two or three *other* people, your secondary support system—because what you're going to need in the weeks to come will be too much of a burden for just one person.

One of the great things about women is that we have friends. We have the possibility of support systems. Men usually don't.

But again, a caution: remember that the people who show up to support you are not *necessarily* going to be your former dear friends. One or two of those may offer such a cockamamie excuse as "Little Jennie is playing soccer, so I'm really too busy right now." When you need blood, the people who turn out to donate aren't always the ones you expect. Don't worry too much about who says yes or no—just concentrate on getting your support crew.

Some dumpees say the best thing that can happen during this period is to connect with another woman or women in the same boat. If you don't know one, they suggest, ask friends if *they* have a friend who has been dumped. Get a name, pick up the phone, introduce yourself, and ask if she'd like to meet for coffee to compare notes. There are the obvious benefits of the misery-loves-company camaraderie and the opportunity to swap useful tips about how to cope. But there's also the possibility of new and fine friendships that will sustain you long after you're past your worst stage.

Says one woman: "When my husband left, I didn't know anyone else who was going through something like this or who had ever gone through it. I was terrified. A friend kept saying to me, 'You really should meet so-and-so. Her husband left her last year.' It took me about three weeks to make the call—I just felt embarrassed and sort of ashamed. Finally I did call her, she knew two others, and somehow or other we all got together.

"We all wanted to talk about it. We had our kitchen table sessions and our coffee shop lunches. We were all also seeing professional counselors—I think friends can only do so much. But these women and I had such a good connection, and we helped one another along, and we're all still together, getting on with our lives, still having a good time. So I'd say this is essential: find somebody in the same situation."

2) **Steer clear of the man who just dumped you.**

You're thinking about him constantly. You can't believe he *really* meant it when he said it was over. You're sure you can convince him you do belong together. You're desperate to hear his voice. You want to know where he is this minute, at ten o'clock Tuesday night.

Right now you will not be able to stop yourself from thinking about him. But you *must* stop yourself during these early days from taking any action to talk to, see, or in any other way be in touch with him.

Don't call your ex and try to start a conversation.

Don't call him and hang up when he answers.

Don't call when you know you'll get his machine, just to hear his voice.

Don't send him a friendship card, even one with a message that you've decided (after looking at every card in the shop) sounds appropriately interested but not desperate, neutral but not distant, caring but not mushy.

Don't call because you left something of yours at his place. One woman left a message on her ex-boyfriend's machine saying she'd like to stop over and pick up her bike helmet, and would he call and let her know when she could come by. The next day the helmet was delivered to her apartment by messenger. She was mortified because, although she did want the helmet back, what she wanted even more was an excuse to see him—and clearly he didn't want to see her.

Don't plan how you can "accidentally" run into him.

Just stop all this. When you can't keep your hand off the phone, dial your support person instead and tell her how miserable you feel. If she's on the job, she'll remind you that for now you must concentrate on getting out of your walking wounded stage, and talking to him is the last thing that will help you do that. She'll also point out (loyal, tough-love support person that she is) that if he said he's leaving or he doesn't love you anymore or in any other way made it known that he wants out, you won't change his mind by anything you might say to him right now. So don't bring upon yourself more agony and possible humiliation by going after him.

For now, screen calls through your machine, and if he phones, don't answer. Don't return his call. There's a slight possibility that he's had a change of heart, come to his senses, and wants to get back together—but *slight* is the operative word. Almost surely he's feeling guilty, and he doesn't like that, and he's calling now to say, "How're things? How are you doing?" Why should you help him believe he's really a nice guy after all? If he wants you back, you'll find out.

In Chapter 3, we offer advice on how to conduct any future relationship with your ex—and if property, divorce, or children are part of the picture, you will have to talk to or see him at times. Ideally, in these early days and weeks while you're still critically wounded, you should have nothing to do with the guy. If you see/talk to him now, he will be either chilly and indifferent, and you'll be further crushed, or pleasant and sweet, and you'll get your hopes up, which you shouldn't. Try to think of him as dead.

3) **See a doctor, lawyer, and therapist.**

First, the doctor. Go to your trusty GP or internist, tell him or her what's happened, get your blood pressure checked, get weighed in, and get some advice about vitamins and nutrition. A doctor visit may seem like an unnecessary bit of business—and an expense you can do without right now. It isn't. Consider your doctor a useful ally.

(Do not, however, jump at a doctor's suggestion that sleeping pills are what you need. If given that advice, find another doctor. Sleeping pills will make you feel as if you're walking on sponges. And even if you take the pills and get your sleep, you'll still have to wake up and deal with the rotten situation you're in.)

The fact is, a lover's betrayal hurts your body as well as your heart and soul. Some women, like Janice, get really sick: "I had a complete physical shutdown. About two or three days after I got dumped, I went out for dinner and a movie with my parents. In the theater I started to get itchy. After the movie my folks went home. I went home, took off my clothes, and my entire body was covered in hives. I went to the emergency room and then to a dermatologist, and they decided that I had a mild allergy to something and my body was refusing to fight it. I was having an allergy to my life!

"I ended up on very strong cortisone-type medication, which knocked me out for a month so that my body could heal. I was a mess—couldn't go to work, couldn't do anything. My parents had to move in and take care of me.

"In retrospect I think it was almost fortunate that I got so sick. I equate it with hitting rock bottom, so I had nowhere to go but up. I got better, I got out of bed, I went back to work."

Says Val: "You can't really overemphasize the unbelievable pain when you find out someone you love has betrayed you to this level. You feel there is poison oozing out of every pore. You are filled with bile that this person could do such a thing to you. You have no appetite. Your heart starts pounding at odd times. The guy has poisoned you, and your poor body is reacting to that poison. You feel so horribly ill!"

Chances are that physically you will feel vulnerable and low if not sick. You will eat strangely or not at all. So check in with your doctor and consider him or her part of your tertiary support team.

Second, if the man who has just dumped you is your husband, or if you and your former lover have shared financial interests, see a lawyer. Right away. On the same day you see your doctor.

We will not go into chapter and verse here about how to negotiate a divorce. Books exist, complete with forms and checklists, to advise on that, and you should buy one as soon as you are enough out of your walking wounded stage to get to a bookstore and read titles. It's wise to inform yourself to the limit because you do not want to turn these important details over to a legal adviser, no matter how astute, blindly.

In these first days, however, a fact-finding visit with a lawyer is crucial. While you're still reeling from emotional shock, the guy who's just walked out on you is very possibly figuring out whether he can get the divorce before or after next year's taxes, or he may be transferring titles to cars and houses. In fact, the occasional dumpee has learned that her former mate was *way* ahead of her in arranging the financial affairs of their recently joint life to his advantage and her misery. Even if he is telling you all will be well, you don't need a lawyer, you can have everything, don't believe him. See a lawyer.

Call the savviest friend you know—ideally, a woman who's been through the same mill you're entering—and ask for a recommendation. If you don't know any savvy people, call your local bar association.

Have an exploratory meeting. At this point you don't need to draw up a major battle plan, and the lawyer you see may not be the one you stick with for the long haul. In the course of a one or two hour meeting, you should review some of your options and establish some of your rights—can your dumper force the sale of your house, for example.

Just minimally, you will be wise to take basic self-preservation precautions, such as making sure the insurance policies are up to date in case a brick falls on your ex. (You think it's only fair that a brick *should* fall on him, although in fact, bricks never seem to fall on guys like this; they have a bullet-proof quality that defies justice.)

Says Barbara: "One of Bob's best friends was the one who came to my rescue. Guy is himself a lawyer. He learned that Bob had left me, and the same day he called me—he actually tracked me down and had me paged—and he said, 'You have to get a lawyer, and you have to get one fast, on Monday morning.' I wasn't ready for this, wasn't thinking that way. If I thought about it at all, I assumed that everything would be split fifty-fifty. But Guy was adamant. I did what he said, and later Guy and the lawyer got me organized. They told me not to rush or settle early. Really, they saved me. Otherwise I wouldn't have a dime today."

Later in this book we have more experiences to share and suggestions to make on the subject of your legal counsel. For now just remember to talk to one soonest, if only to establish your rights.

Finally, your therapist. Almost every dumpee we have talked to says that a brief (for some, a long-term) period of professional counseling was invaluable in the walking wounded stage or later.

One woman feels that *not* seeking such help was one of the biggest mistakes she made: "I was the kind of person who'd never consider getting a shrink. I just thought, I'm strong, I'm intelligent and educated, I had a good childhood and upbringing, I'll get through this by myself. You really can't get through it by yourself. Or even if you can, why should you when you can get someone to help you?"

Another woman found herself surrounded by concerned friends who were intent on jollying her out of her woundedness, which she says was sweet and dear but not what she needed: "It's as if you have a bad fall down a flight of steps, and people rush to get you standing on your feet again when that's the exact wrong thing to do. When you're dumped, your friends are enormously supportive, but it's great to talk to somebody who's trained to help you handle what's happening.

"I remember walking into the office of the psychologist I started seeing at that time and saying 'OK, the thing is I am losing my mind. I am going insane.' And she very calmly said, 'Really? What makes you think so? What's going on?' I saw her for five or six sessions, and at the end she said, 'You're not insane. I have watched you progressing through very normal steps of grieving, and you're OK.' And you know, I thought, Great! That's all I needed from her at that time. Before talking to her, I was pretty sure I was cooked, no one else had been through this, and I was never going to get better."

Things may be going on in your mind that you can't comfortably talk about with a friend, even your primary support person. Or your loving, sympathetic pals may buoy you up but not keep you moving forward. That's what a little therapy can do for you at a time when your perspective may be out of whack, you're confused, and your emotions are seesawing wildly. A counselor can help calm you down, validate your feelings, and organize your thoughts. "Getting this kind of professional help," says one woman, "would be my number one suggestion for any woman who's just been dumped—with ten stars next to it."

Finding such a person is not difficult. Your GP will be able to make a reference. So will your minister or rabbi. Ask around, or look in the phone book for family service associations that can recommend counseling to fit your needs and budget.

4) **Avoid taking drastic actions.**

This is something you're probably hearing from your doctor, lawyer, therapist, or support person, and it's good advice.

Don't decide this is the time to pull up stakes and get a job tending bar in Maui.

Don't be rushed into a divorce.

Don't sell your home, unless you absolutely have to.

You're not in good enough shape at the moment to make large decisions rationally.

5) **Do not overeat or undereat.**

You're likely to do one or the other, and obviously neither is great. Though some women may ease their misery by scarfing down cake and pizza, we haven't met a lot of those.

Cynthia's story seems par for the course: "I stopped eating. I didn't even realize it. I would go home after work and have a bag of popcorn and a glass of wine and go to bed. I lost twenty-five pounds in three months and looked like a hag."

And Maggie's: "My friends told me later they could see me wasting away. You stop making meals."

And Susan's: "I lived on bananas."

If you have been needing to shed a few pounds, such unforced weight loss may seem like one of the rare bonuses to come along with the pain. But the Dumped Diet is not recommended.

Eat at least fairly decently in order not to get sick and look anorexic. Get multivitamins. When a friend calls and asks if you need anything, ask her to bring over some takeout or a piece of apple pie or to drag you out for lunch or to go for a walk with you. Exercise is good.

Sometimes return to your childhood comfort foods to make yourself feel cosseted and food seem appealing. When you're in an especially bad funk, you might indulge yourself with your old favorites—mashed potatoes with lots of butter, rice pudding, macaroni and cheese, strawberry ice cream. This is not a balanced diet, of course, but it won't do you irreparable harm. You'll feel comforted, and it's better than not eating at all.

6) **Don't drink alone.**

It's easy right now to become a drunk. Liquor, says one woman who learned the hard way, is the handmaiden of loneliness.

If you're telling yourself it's OK because you only drink between the hours of 6 and 7:30 P.M.—and if at the same time you find yourself *really* looking forward to 6 and *really* regretting 7:30—you might be heading for trouble.

When you feel the need for a drink after work, when you feel you damn well deserve one for getting through a day, invite a friend to join you. A casual acquaintance is fine, too. If you've always enjoyed your wine, never open a bottle on your own in the early days of being dumped. Ask someone over for an impromptu dinner, even someone you're not that eager to see, and *then* have some wine.

7) **Let yourself wallow.**

This is important. Now is no time for a stiff upper lip, and it's definitely no time for major denial. You are hurt. You are unhappy. You feel like crying (and crying produces endorphins that make you feel better).

So do cry and wallow—but set limits.

Suppose you have a low—a *very* low—day. Say to yourself, "I'm going to spend this whole evening thinking about it all and being completely miserable. Then I'm going to stop when it's time for the eleven o'clock news. I'm going to watch the news, and then I'm going to go to bed and to sleep."

You *can* have that kind of self-control. If you find yourself sliding into a wallow in the middle of the afternoon when you've got to get things accomplished and you can't afford one, say, *"Stop! Not now!"* Interrupt the tape starting to play again in your head; save it for later.

Maybe you'll find as time goes along that you don't even need all the wallow time you've set aside for yourself.

Says Ginny: "When it first happens, just be true to what you feel like doing. It's really OK if you want to stay in your pajamas for two days, maybe even for two weeks. For a lot of women the instinct is to do what they think they 'should' do: be brave, be tough, soldier on. And then at some period down the road, four months or six or a year, they kind of crash and burn because they never let themselves just grieve. I've seen that happen to two friends.

"You've got to be unhappy. You've got to mope for a while because it is a shitty thing that has just happened. So do it. But have somebody watching so that you don't go on for too long or you don't go right over the top."

Obviously you will have to keep up with some of the business of real life, primarily your job and your children if you have one or both. One woman says that for a year she woke up every morning at seven, got her kids up and out to school, went to work, home at six, and straight to bed. She told her children, who were young teenagers, "Make dinner. I can't do it." A couple of hours later she'd get up, have something to eat, wash her face, brush her teeth, and go back to bed. It was a time, she says, during which she had no strength or energy for more than the absolute basics of her day.

If you need to function minimally for a while, do so. As long as children and pets are fed and otherwise cared for, you and everyone else *will* survive.

8) Hurl yourself into a mindless task.

This is the flip side of sitting motionless on your couch having a good wallow, and some newly dumped women report finding healthy escape in tackling a massive, if unnecessary, project.

Take every book you own off the bookshelves, oil or repaint the shelves, look at each book, put the ones you don't want to keep in a box to go to a charity, and (after the shelves have dried) put the rest back up alphabetized by author. Run out to your local home supply store and buy plastic storage bins, expanding rods, and zippy wallpaper. Go home, empty your closet, then wallpaper it. Install the rods and bins, and put all your clothes back obsessively organized by style, length, and color.

On days when you are too wounded to venture far from home, do something that keeps you busy, occupies your hands, doesn't take too much thought, and kills time—if you're so inclined and the spirit moves you.

9) **Avoid self-inflicted pain.**

Listen only to nonassociative music. Love songs will derail you for a whole day. No country. Try classical. Even if you connect it with your time together, classical music doesn't seem to push the same buttons as Barbra singing "The Way We Were" or Whitney warbling "Didn't We Almost Have It All?"

Think about your personal button pushers. If your former man sang "I'll Be Loving You, Always" at the surprise thirty-fifth birthday party he threw for you (because it was a song you heard the night you met), this is clearly a tune you want to avoid. In the journal you may decide to keep, write down all your button pushers, and know you've got to eliminate these reminders of a time that's gone from your life—at least until you're stronger.

In these early weeks, avoid restaurants, galleries, parks, laundromats, or wherever you routinely went as a couple. You don't want to churn up those memories, and you *definitely* don't want to chance running into him.

Avoid looking at pictures of happier times. Put these and all other mementos, letters, and any other items connected to your joint life into a carton, and stash the carton in the remote recesses of your hall closet or your storage bin in the basement—not under your bed where it will be easy to pull out, wade through, and mope over. Later, when you're better, you'll look at the carton's contents and decide what you want to do with them.

10) Get something to hug.

Buy a soft stuffed animal or one of those four-foot-long pillows to take to bed at night—you need something cuddly to hold on to.

This can also take some of the pressure off your long-suffering support person on those nights when you can't do anything but sit there and mope. Just hold your stuffed bear, stare at the TV, and let go.

11) Look as good as you can.

Keep up your appearance. If you've always had your roots done and nails polished, continue to do so.

Do not, however, get an eye lift right now. You don't need to be recovering from surgery in addition to everything else. For another thing, an eye lift changes the way tears come forth. Instead of running down the cheeks, tears shoot forward horizontally, as if off little diving boards. This is disconcerting to you and others and makes it difficult to wear sunglasses, so wait until you're out of your most weepy stage before you consider tightening the lids.

In the immediate aftermath of being dumped, some women feel a powerful motivation, even compulsion, to work out in earnest. If you are one of them, great—he's shipped out, but at least you can shape up. Buy an aerobics video, or leave the office, proceed directly to your local Y, and take a swim. What Scandinavians call "the blue hour," that time of evening before darkness settles in and while the sky is a provocative shade of violet, is a heartbreaker. Spend it at a gym.

12) Make lists.

If you've never been a list maker, start now. If you've been a compulsive one all your adult life, keep at it. It helps a lot to have before you physical, visible evidence of what is or will or should be happening each day and in the weeks ahead.

One woman says that in her walking wounded stage she was able to plan ahead in no greater than fifteen-minute segments. She knew she was getting better when that increased to hours and then days. Lists will help you get there by organizing the jumble in your head and relieving some pressures.

Separate your short-term decisions into categories and put dates on them. If you've got "Refinance mortgage?" or "Send for business school applications?" on your list of decisions and it's a nonemergency item you can think about or check into three months from now, put a date on it and forget about it in the meantime.

While you're at it, make a list of friends or activities you've let fall by the wayside—maybe because *he* didn't approve—that you'd like to get back to. Make a list of fifty things you want to do before you die (buy an Armani suit, live in a place with a potting shed, spend a week at a Benedictine retreat, sail to Bali). You don't have to take action on any of them at the moment, but you'll benefit from seeing before you in black and white these options and dreams, markers toward a newly active and rewarding life.

13) Start a journal.

Many women have been helped by recording their thoughts and feelings. If you think you might be one of them (even if you don't, give it a try), buy a notebook and begin at once: "Friday, April 10. I am in the slough of despond. . . ."

Try to write something in your journal every day during these first weeks. Do not go back and read what you have written, however, for at least three months. Later you're going to take a look at it, and you're going to be pleasantly surprised because you will see how much stronger you've become.

Says Elizabeth: "I got a notebook, and I started writing in it sporadically, not every day. This is so cathartic when your life is an emotional fog. You couldn't call it a diary. It wasn't a catalog of events, just random thoughts. I wrote what I felt. Sometimes I was in tears, and sometimes I was quite happy, so it got a bit lopsided. Where it was terribly useful was going back and reading over things months later and seeing the benchmarks, where I started from and the place I had reached. It's therapy—also a wonderful way to have a good cry, if you want, when no one's around to listen."

Write a hateful letter to your ex if you have an urge to vent, a letter you wish you could but of course will not mail to him. Do not be surprised, however, if you find yourself writing instead the love letter to end all love letters. While you're still reeling in disbelief and pain, still hoping this is a bad dream, you may focus on what was wonderful about him—what you long to have back. Write away. Later on you will be able to see him and your past relationship in better balance and a clearer light.

If no thoughts come to mind, here are some suggestions to get you started on your journal. Complete the following:

I can't believe that someone who once loved me would—

I will stop obsessing about the following "minor actions" of his—

In the last week I have done the following to encourage new people to enter my life—

In the last week I have done the following to make me feel a little better, even if only for a few minutes at a time—

I will plan the following activities for next week to give me something to look forward to—

To maintain my health I have started—

When I felt really down in the past, I started to feel better when I—

Here are some activities I can manage at this point that will benefit someone else and maybe make me feel better about myself—

Even if money is tight, I can make the following changes in my home to remove reminders of him—

Writing in a journal is great when you're awake at three in the morning, and it's good for the soul. Don't torture yourself over it. Just write stuff down, so it's not all happening only in your mind. Stash those hopes, dreams, and plans in your journal, too.

14) Develop a mantra.

You understand now the concept *dying of a broken heart*. But you are *not* going to die. You are *not* going to let this person do that to you. As much as you loved him and devoted yourself to him, you won't let him destroy your life.

That's your mantra—put it in words that have meaning for you. As you lie in bed at night, say it to yourself. Tape record it, add passages you like from books or poetry that give you hope and motivation, and play your tape as you're drifting off. This is a kind of self-hypnosis, and it will do you good.

15) Try hard not to obsess.

You hear that your ex-man took his new woman to the restaurant you two used to frequent, and you turn this fact over and over in your mind.

You will learn over time that nothing about your past life together is sacred to the man who dumped you. He'll take the new woman out to your favorite restaurant, order your favorite dinner, *and* ask the piano player to play your favorite song. This behavior doesn't seem bizarre to him, because men, unlike us, have a remarkable capacity to compartmentalize their lives. What was then was then, what is now is now, and the one has nothing to do with the other.

You obsess about these small betrayals because you cannot yet handle the big betrayal. And you go over and over and over them in your mind.

Try to limit this kind of conversation in your own head, and if it's out loud, *definitely* keep it for your primary support person.

16) **Plan a trip.**

Although you may not be ready or can't afford to get out of town, you can *think* about doing so. Read the travel pages in your Sunday newspaper, call the phone number for further information on the Tuscany tour, ask for brochures, start a folder. Entertain the possibility of escape.

17) **Buy yourself a daily treat.**

Taking a stroll and smelling the flowers or looking out over the ocean and watching the seagulls is all to the good. Find these or other small ways to be kind to yourself and appreciate the finer things in nature. But in addition, buy yourself a small something, as much as you can afford, every day. It's important at this juncture to spend money on yourself.

If you're coming out of a long-term marriage, money will almost surely loom large, probably unpleasantly so, in the weeks, months, or years to come. It may be a source of great anxiety and a bone of great contention. Get in a mental state that says, "I'm entitled to money; I can spend it on myself."

Says Sara: "A good friend—he was, in fact, an usher at our wedding—called me when he heard that Jon had left, and he was not amused by what Jon had done. At the end of our conversation, Gary said to me, 'Buy yourself a treat every day. It doesn't matter how small it is. Just do it.' The next day I left for work a little earlier than usual, and I stopped in a lovely little pastry shop in my neighborhood. I had a cappuccino and read the paper. Now I do that every day. While the cappuccino is expensive, every time I buy it it gives me a lift."

18) Get massages.

This is a great way to spend money on yourself.

Says Marcia: "Before this I had never had a massage, a facial, a pedicure. A friend talked me into it, and I went to the best spa in town and had all those things done. On the way home I bought a shower massage. All this helped me more than I can say. I spent a pile and had a heart attack three weeks later when the bill arrived, but it was worth it."

If your budget is tight, get one massage or as many as you can afford. You have suffered a physical loss—sexually, of course, but you have also lost the comfort of casually hugging and touching the man you were with for a long time.

It's a scientific fact that women have more nerve endings at the surface of the skin than men do. We *need* to be touched. And massages are relaxing and a lot safer than stumbling into an inappropriate affair because you feel lonely and touch-deprived.

19) Sleep on his side of the bed.

If you're there, you won't be on *your* side feeling his absence. Or maybe you always wanted to be on that side anyway but let him have it. Now's your chance.

Says Toni: "The night Fred left I just went to bed. The next morning my daughter came down the hall into my room, and she said, 'What are you doing sleeping on that side of the bed?' I hadn't thought about it, but there I was. I looked and I said, 'You know, I've always wanted to sleep over here.'"

20) Forget about men for now.

For the first year, avoid trying to find someone else.

Do not decide to call up an old boyfriend in an attempt to rekindle an old spark. If he's polite and yet clearly disinterested, you'll feel foolish. If he tells you he's involved with someone or, worse, married, you'll feel foolish *and* devastated.

Be cautious about accepting a date. You are on such rocky ground right now, you will be inclined either to pounce on any flaw in the man as an excuse to flee or to overlook everything that's clearly wrong. You will inevitably compare the new man, for good or bad, to your ex, and you'll be unable to see him clearly.

Don't go out with someone new in the hope that word will get back to your ex.

If you have an old male pal to take in a movie with occasionally, fine. Otherwise, skip men.

Other People (Friends, Enemies, Crowd Scenes, Your Mother, His Mother . . .)

What They Will Say, What You Should Say

Let's suppose that getting the news you're being dumped for another woman comes as an odd kind of release. Suppose that suddenly life makes sense again, as if you're coming out of a long foggy haze and can see—if still only dimly—a clearer, better path ahead. For two or three women we've talked to, that's what happened.

Beth says: "When I got a phone call telling me that he was sleeping with another woman, I felt as if a thousand pounds had been lifted off my shoulders. I wasn't paranoid, as he had been leading me to believe for months. I had a brain. I was normal. All those suspicions I'd had for a long time were true. All those denials he had made were false. All the comments about what was wrong with me were for his own purposes. And I don't think I have ever looked back."

But even when you realize that the other shoe

has finally dropped and you can get on with it, you cringe.

Beth continues: "He left on the first of January, and I felt that I was standing nude in Times Square. He had just exposed our private little family to the world. There was going to be gossip and talk and people to tell and sides taken. It's just so damn embarrassing to have everybody know your husband has left you."

There *is* going to be talk, and sides will be taken. Some friends will take you under their wing in wonderful ways. Some friends you won't hear from, maybe ever again. If you're being dumped by a husband, there may be a reshuffling of family alliances.

People may give you bad advice or say dumb things. To some in the immediate aftermath of getting dumped, you may become a problem, a threat, or an object of pity or curiosity. You're in an awkward situation that your ex has caused through his own voluntary action—but you're the one who's embarrassed and uncomfortable.

This is certainly not fair, but there it is, so it behooves you to get over your fury, face the embarrassment, and handle what comes at you with all the finesse and class you can muster.

Who, What, and When to Tell

Ideally you have your support person or persons in place, the one(s) you can talk to with all stops open.

Some women, though, aren't sure how to get the word out about what's happened. Dumpees we've talked to ran the gamut from announcing it to the world to keeping a zipped lip.

Says one: "I let it all hang out in the beginning because I was just destroyed. I didn't *quite* stand on street corners and tell anyone who walked by. But I did tell close friends, not-so-close friends, family, my boss—basically anybody who'd listen and, you know, understand."

Says another: "I didn't tell a soul when he left. After a while my mother caught me in a lie, so I did let her know. But I didn't want to tell people, because a lot was going through my head. For one thing, everybody thought Bob was so great, and it sounded unbelievable to say, 'He's having an affair.' And I suppose I thought, too, Maybe this will all work out and we'll get back together, and I don't want to upset my parents."

Somewhere in between those two stances is your best way to go. Don't stand on street corners announcing that you've been dumped. When the dry cleaner or the fruit stand guy says, "Hi, how's it going?" you don't want to reply, "Hi, my boyfriend left me." Don't make your unhappiness and anger your sole topic of conversation.

Says Bev: "You've got to be a grown-up. The huge mistake many women make is to buttonhole everyone with their side of the whole acrimonious business. Acrimony isn't attractive. They cut themselves off—nobody wants to hear all this. Ninety-five percent of the people who say, 'How are you?' want you to reply you're just fine. Share the good things in your life. Don't bore your friends with your woes. When I really need somebody to talk to, I go to a counselor. I want somebody I can *pay* to listen to me."

At the same time, don't bury the news deep within you while you put on a business-as-usual demeanor. The sooner you let the pertinent people in your world know, the sooner you can move beyond it, the sooner any embarrassment you're feeling will fade, and the more control you will have over any gossip that ensues.

Besides, if you're unwilling to tell another living soul, that's probably an indication that you feel totally responsible and deficient or that you think this is a temporary glitch and it will all blow over.

Says one dumpee: "A lot of women don't talk about it in the beginning because they think the guy will come back, so there's no point in telling anyone. I kept it quiet for months because he and I did continue to work together and go to company functions together, which was an impossible situation now that I think about it. So I was just waiting to see what happened next. That was a big mistake and a waste of time."

Let people know, because:

• They'll find out anyway, and it's better that they hear it from you.

Merilee says: "At the time I thought keeping it to myself was the best decision for me. But later I learned my family was hurt and annoyed that I didn't let them know. If I had to do it again, I'd probably tell everyone right away."

- You will get support, even from unexpected corners.

Merilee says that her boss and other coworkers found out about her divorce only after she submitted a name change (from her hyphenated married name to her single name) for the company phone directory: "I was so surprised at the reaction. A lot of people stopped me in the hall or phoned and just said, 'I'm really sorry about what's going on.' My supervisor was very sweet and protective. It was encouraging."

So let people know—beginning with family.

Your Family

Many women say their mothers, fathers, sisters, or brothers were at hand and on call from the beginning, to give them emotional support and, often, practical help at a time when they weren't thinking too clearly.

One or more of these closest relatives may be your primary support person or on the team. One woman says: "My boyfriend, Steve, left me for a woman named Karen. Karen had been living with Paul, so Paul also got dumped. One of the stranger things that happened during this time of what I can only describe as my mental aberration was that Paul and I started talking a lot, usually, of course, about Steve and Karen. And I began to imagine myself madly in love with Paul!

"During this period of about three months, I called my brother every afternoon at his office. Every single afternoon. He'd listen to me ramble on for a half hour, and then he'd calmly, gently stop me, in effect, from doing something really half-cocked, such as giving up my apartment and getting one in the complex where Paul lived."

Says Deirdre: "I've always been a religious person, but during that time I think I kind of gave up my religion because I was so devastated. It was my relatives and family, especially my brother's wife, who helped me through. She spent a lot of time with me then, and I remember her saying 'You are in a lot of pain and you can't sidestep it. It's a tunnel. You have to look through it and go on through it, and there's a light at the end.' I actually was able to visualize that, and it helped."

You may discover, like several of the dumpees we've talked to, that along with support and love comes a new mutual appreciation. One woman took her mother out to lunch to tell her about the separation: "To my surprise, my mother described to me a similar experience she had years ago, before she met my dad." They talked, she says, as two adult women sharing thoughts and emotions and since then have relished the added closeness that has developed between them.

If you have loving family members in your life who will commiserate *and* help to keep your head screwed on straight, be grateful and use them. If you have loving family members who are likely to go to pieces themselves over this upheaval you're in, tell them the news while keeping a healthy distance. This is a time to remain fixed on your own recovery, and you shouldn't have to deal with someone else's worries, disappointments, or jangled nerves—for example, your mother's.

You know your mother. Will she be a brick or a basket case? If it's a basket case, break the news to her immediately and simply, cutting off for the moment any emotional outbursts or long talks that will just fuel your own unhappiness.

Most likely she has had no clue that all was not well with your love life, because you gave her none. Perhaps she saw you and your ex only intermittently, when you were both on your best behavior. Now she will be surprised and upset. She may want to talk you out of "breaking up" and urge you to "try harder." This you don't need.

Call and say, for example, "Mom, I want you to know that George has left me for another woman, and while I know I have your love and support, I'm just too upset right now to discuss it. I love you, and we'll talk again soon."

His Family

Susan got the news that she was being dumped and—like a Stepford wife, she says—went ahead as planned to her in-laws' house for drinks to celebrate her husband's birthday: "Doug and I and his parents were sitting there, and the three of them were chatting away normally. I was in shock. I decided I deserved a martini. Then I had another one. Then I said to his mother, 'Has your son told you that he's moving out of our home tomorrow?' Doug turned white. His mother, amazingly, said, 'Why are you telling me this now and ruining his birthday?' I said, 'Well, you know, he's just ruined my life, so why not?'"

The two-martini bombshell announcement may not be the best idea, but if you have at least a semi-friendly relationship with his parents, it's wise to let them know shortly after the dumping. You don't want them hearing it from other people, and your ex-man may put off this bit of business as long as he can get away with it, which only complicates your life.

Call your in-laws. Say: "I imagine you've heard that George has left. Needless to say, I'm devastated and sad, but I value your friendship, and I hope it will continue." Take the high road, in other words. Don't say to her, "Boy, did you give birth to a worm!"

Don't assume that you're losing people who have meant a lot to you over the years. If you have had a solid, affectionate relationship with your ex-man's parents or other family, if they are struggling to come to grips with the love they naturally feel for their son and the dismay they may feel for his recent actions, the chances are good that you will continue to enjoy their support, admiration, or friendship.

A dumpee whose husband left her literally homeless and unable to pay rent was put up by *his* parents for as long as she needed to find an apartment and get on her feet again. Other women report similarly positive reactions.

Says Erica: "The interesting thing to me is that the people who were most helpful to me, beyond my close friends, were Scott's family. They were absolutely fabulous and still are today. I've had wonderful, heartfelt conversations with my former in-laws about the difficulty they have in trying to accept Scott's new wife and not allowing themselves to care about her too much. They say that emotionally it would be painful for them if Scott does to the new wife what he did to me. So, oddly, I find myself talking about his wife, a person whose well-being I certainly am not losing sleep over. I do, however, care for my in-laws, and they let me know they care for me, and I feel we're helping each other."

Another woman has kept in contact with her former mother-in-law for over fifteen years: "Bill's mother, who is old now, has through all the years phoned me regularly. And she's just been superb about me. She always asks about the kids and what's going on with them and then invariably says something that means, 'I think you're doing a great job, carry on.'"

On the other hand, don't assume that your in-laws will find you blameless. If your relationship with the ex-man's family *hasn't* been too sunny, or if they're bound to justify any rotten deed their princeling might pull off, you'll feel the heat. Don't attempt to change their minds. If you have children, do the minimum you must do to maintain cordial family relations. If you're hearing semislanderous remarks coming from those quarters, set the record straight, still keeping to the high road.

Here's how Emma handled things: "His mother was running around talking to joint friends, also to my mom and dad, and saying essentially that it takes two to tango and Emma was just too caught up in her career to be a good wife and so on.

"When I hear this kind of thing I say to people, 'I should and I will take my share of responsibility in the marriage breakdown. But I don't take responsibility for Bob's affair. That was his choice and his choice entirely, to go outside our marriage and resolve whatever issues were troubling him.' I think they get the message."

When you're being dumped from a marriage, especially one of some duration and especially one that produced children, your soon-to-be ex-relatives will almost surely be rattled by the end of what they assumed or chose to assume was a happy couple. If you are genuinely fond of them and hope to stay in touch, tell them so. Examine your motives carefully, however. Do not perpetuate these connections and conversations to encourage *them* to work on *him* to come back to you. It *won't* work.

Be as honest as possible without trashing your ex; they are, after all, *his* people, and you'll only come off looking bad if you run down a list of his sins. Maybe you've always had great good times with his sister, and maybe you will again although on different grounds. Or maybe you won't; blood runs thick. It will be a while before all this shakes down.

The World at Large

When you're getting a bit bored with licking your wounds or fanning the flames of your rage, when you've unburdened yourself to your support team and they're shoring you up, when your primary support person is insisting you come out to a little dinner party or a big bash or get back on the softball team, then you're ready for social outings.

Here is where you make a distinction between your private (good buddies, primary support team) and your more public self. Let down your hair with the support team; keep it up on the general social scene. Publicly you want to maintain control and some sense of humor. If you think you *really* can't yet handle going out and trying to be light, don't go. You might need more time moping with your stuffed bear after all.

When you do meet the world at large, here are some things that may happen.

You're Stunned at People's Reactions to the Dumping

The reactions that flabbergast you come in one of two ways:

- Friends or coworkers or your neighbors tell you they've seen your ex out and about with another woman, and all this is *no surprise at all*.

During the weeks Tonya was hearing less and less from her boyfriend of four years and seeing him hardly at all, she believed his explanations that he had to be on the road a lot right now. She knew for a fact that he attended a sales training seminar in Belgium for several days because she called his office and was told he was at a conference in Europe and because he sent her a postcard from Bruges. Later, after he dumped her, she learned the rest of the story: "He was at the conference. He was also over there with his new girlfriend. Most of our friends knew this. It seemed everybody knew this except me."

Some dumpees coming out of long-term marriages start hearing in dribs and drabs about a series of infidelities on their ex's part. "The last woman is the one who's still on board," says Carol, "but apparently there were at least three others over the past twelve years. A couple of our friends were aware of this, and they're telling me they've known for a long time that he's a cheater."

- People tell you they *can't believe it*—they thought you and he were a solid gold couple.

One woman says she and everybody else thought hers was one great little family: "My daughter's friends used to say to her, 'I wish I had your mother, I wish I had your father, I love your house.' When Jack left me, people told me it was like a bolt from the blue. They said they used to be envious at what a close marriage we had. Even the maitre d' at the restaurant he and I used to go to a lot made a point of telling me how sorry he was that we weren't together, that it had always been a pleasure to see us there since we always had so much to talk to each other about. A lot of good all this does me now."

Either observation—I knew it was going to happen or I can't believe it happened—leaves you at a loss for words because you're wondering if everything in the life you so recently lived was a lie and a sham.

You must make some response, but what?

It will be better for your recovery and your role as a social being in the world at large if you manage to keep that response simple, noncommittal, even a bit lofty.

- When someone says she knew all about the other woman or "he's been playing around for years," she probably thinks you'll feel less of a failure if you know what a rat your ex is. In fact, she's right, although it will be difficult for you to appreciate it as you listen to her spill the beans.

If you've been carrying around a rosy picture of the time you and your ex were together, blaming yourself that it's over, and hoping maybe you can get it back, part of your recovery involves letting go of that picture and those feelings. You must construct a new, realistic picture of your relationship as one that included significant deception.

Additionally, if you're looking toward divorce, it may be to your benefit to know about your ex's infidelities.

So listen to the distressing information, and suffer through the embarrassment of realizing that virtual strangers knew details about your most intimate relationship that you didn't. Later go home and write all this in your journal, and call your support person and rant to her about your anger and hurt.

To the person telling you all this, say simply: "Well, I suppose I can understand why you kept that information from me until now. Live and learn, huh?"

- When someone says you could have knocked her over with a feather when she heard the news because you and he were such a dynamite pair, try not to burst into tears or say you can't believe it either, there'll never be another love for you, you want to kill him, and you want to kill yourself. She'll think you're pathetic, and later you'll think you're pathetic, too.

Instead, bite your tongue and say: "Well, the end of a relationship is always sad, and now I'm looking ahead to the future."

You Walk into a Room Full of People and Conversation Stops Cold

If for some time you and your ex were a solid couple solidly ensconced in a circle of friends or business associates, it will happen. When it does, don't hesitate to use the word *dumped*. It's what all those people who stop talking and stare at you are thinking, and it's better that *you* say it.

For example, if someone asks, "How are you doing?" reply: "Well, it certainly isn't pleasant being dumped, but I'm trying to remember the good times with George."

People will be surprised to hear these words from you. Such words show that you're coming to grips with what happened—and they'll admire you and the fact that you're not going to make a scene. Plus it's good for you and your recovery to put a name to your condition.

Says one woman: "People would say to me something like 'I'm so sorry to hear that you and Philip are having trouble,' and I'd say, 'Well, I wouldn't call it trouble exactly—I've been dumped.' It made everything a lot easier for me. I think the women who aren't able to confront the word, who say, 'Frank and I are going through a difficult period' and so on, are the ones who are in danger of going on that way for years. Maybe they harbor the dream that somehow or other good old Frank will come back again. They keep it all under wraps because they think it's going to blow over. They get stalled."

You Will, Out of Nowhere, Feel on the Verge of Losing It

It's hard to reemerge in your old crowd as a solo act. You'll be doing fine and then suddenly think you can't take even one more minute of this.

Don't run for the door. Tough it out—you'll be strengthened by your own display of grit and feel more confident in the future. Practice survival techniques:

- If you feel your eyes welling, look up at the ceiling; it helps defuse the tears.
- Do not reach for another drink. Even if you do get teary and talk about the harm that's been done you or in some other way make a spectacle of yourself, people will forgive. If you get drunk, people won't forget and won't ask you back.

Says Jane: "I make my first two drinks plain tonic water with a slice of lime. For my third, I allow myself a tiny splash of vodka. Everybody is at least two drinks ahead of me, which is good."

People Will Encourage You to Speak Ill of the Man Who Has Left You

They may wish to be kind, and they think you'll feel better if they suggest it's all right by them if you want to let off a little steam. Others, not being kind, may be fishing for dirt.

Many dumpees have found that mutual friends, men and women both, are really ticked off at the man's behavior, let him know, and then let her know they've let him know.

Says one: "He lost a lot of respect. One of our friends took him out for coffee and, I think, read him the riot act. She told Tim, 'I don't care what was going on in your head and your pants, you've left a lot of dead bodies in your wake.' She reported this conversation to me afterward."

Says Margot: "I would have guessed that people would go over to Edward's side. That's the control he had over me: Eddie is strong, smart, and right; Margot is meek and wishy-washy. And it absolutely blew me away that everyone has been like my big brother and sister. They know that he shafted me and he's been acting like a rat. And I hear that Edward's nose is out of joint because the guys he used to play poker with don't call him anymore."

All this may give you satisfaction. *Nevertheless*, try as much as you can to say nothing nasty about your ex in public. If others start putting him down, let them go on briefly, and then gracefully close it off. Class and dignity will help you get above it and lead you on to your new life, one that includes some of the old friends who are now dissing him.

One dumpee realized that a lot of talk was going around in her circle concerning the breakup of her marriage and the behavior of her ex: "Shortly after I came out of my really derailed phase, I was at Alfredo's for dinner with three couples, old friends. And another friend who had known Mitch and me stopped at the table to say hello and suddenly was putting Mitch down, saying nasty things about him. I said, 'Peter, I really don't want to have this kind of conversation. I want to concentrate on the good times Mitch and I did have, and I'm not here to put him down.' He was apparently so astounded that he went all over town telling people what I had said."

This kind of remark *does* astound other men, especially his friends or the men you socialized with as a couple; they think you're a class act. And people will be more likely to invite you places than if you sound bitter and talk about how awful George is. Let *them* form the conclusion that he's the bottom of the barrel.

Publicly, in other words, you want to acknowledge that yes you're hurt, but you won't be vicious about it. Remember, you're building a new life for yourself, so be careful not to turn other people off.

People Will Give You Useful Information

Acquaintances and former joint friends who disapprove of your ex-man's shabby behavior may still be privy to what's going on in his life and can tell you things you should know.

One dumpee, whose ex was crying poor, learned from a mutual acquaintance that the guy had recently taken title to a piece of rental real estate. Another heard from a friend that her ex had booked a holiday cruise for himself, the new girl-friend, and her two children.

As with learning about his cheating ways, you probably don't *want* to hear these infuriating or painful bits of news. But they may be useful pieces of information if, for example, you'll be facing a court case over financial settlements. While you're main-taining your dignity and not letting the bad-mouthing get out of hand, it's still wise to keep your ear to the ground and your antennae up. When someone gives you news you can use, say you appre-ciate it.

People Will Say Dumb Things to You

Most people want to be helpful and comforting. Often they don't manage it.

Says one woman: "I think the truth is, people don't know what to say. Years ago I had a miscar-riage, and I remember being surprised about how others reacted. A few people were great and man-aged to say just the right thing. The others either made no mention of it at all—and these were coworkers and neighbors who I knew were aware of what had happened—or they were clumsy, some-times insensitive. Someone might quiz me—how far along was I? did it happen in the hospital? I think they were trying to demonstrate interest but suc-ceeded in making me uncomfortable. Still others said, 'You'll have another baby,' which was also not what I wanted to hear at the moment.

"Now, in this matter of getting dumped, I'm finding the same thing. Some people are terrific and right on. And others, who maybe don't know about traumas in life, are just hopeless."

When people say dumb things to you, you feel pressured. Either you snap back to set the record straight, thereby antagonizing the other person and disliking yourself for sounding hostile. Or you smile, murmur thanks, and seethe inside.

You shouldn't have to suffer fools gladly or rein yourself in to make others feel good for having given forth a supposed kindness. The trick is to set the record straight *without* snapping. You'll feel better, and you'll also be performing a small public service for the soon-to-be dumpees of the world. The individual you're educating may think twice next time before making a thoughtless or painful remark to a wounded woman.

What might you hear? How should you reply?

Seven Dumb Remarks and What to Say Back

1) **"Oh sweetie, how *are* you?"**

There's a certain patronizing tone of voice that suggests the speaker isn't all that concerned with your well-being and in fact might take some small pleasure if you dissolved in tears. To the patronizer, you can lie a little: "I'm doing just fine, thanks for asking."

2) **"What doesn't kill you makes you stronger."**

Says one woman: "I can remember for a long time after it happened I thought to myself—if one more person tells me this is character-building I'm going to punch them."

Reply: "You know, I'm sure you're right about that, but I would have preferred to get my lessons in hard knocks in some other way."

3) **"I ran into George the other day. He looks great [he looks like death warmed over]."**

During these early weeks back in the world again, you don't need these reminders of your ex. (Of course, you're actually *dying* to hear about him, but you should be working at squelching that need.)

The person who tells you your former guy is doing great has a mean streak. The person who tells you he's a mess thinks this news should make you happy (as it does). In either case, don't get into it. You want to convey an attitude that says, "What's going on with George doesn't interest me much anymore." This will help *you* by not aggravating feelings you are trying to get over.

Say: "I guess we'll all run into George for years to come."

4) "I know the pain you're feeling, dear. I've felt it, too."

Widows say this to married dumpees, but in fact they *don't* know and haven't felt. The men they lost would, one assumes, prefer to be alive and with them; the man you lost *is* alive and prefers to be with someone else, and he's probably having a damn good time doing it.

A widow, of course, does feel pain and grief. She does not, however, have to cope with humiliation and insult on top of it all and does not face the distasteful risk of running into her former husband with his new love.

Say to the widow: "I know how much you miss Harry and what a void his death has caused. Of course, though, Harry would *love* to be with you. George, on the other hand, is alive and *doesn't* want to be with me."

This is actually one of the few remarks that makes a widow feel better, so there's a little social work plus here. And at least you won't, for the sake of politeness, accept being coddled in this mistaken way.

5) "You're doing great."

Says Toni: "The comments that most aggravated me were the cheering-up generalizations— you're doing great, or you'll find a new guy, or look how far you've come. These were all very well intended, but nobody was addressing the fact that right now, today, God damn it, I don't feel like I'm doing so great. And right now I don't have somebody to go out to dinner with."

The you're-doing-great, everything's-going-to-be-fine comments come from people who assume it's not going to be that difficult for you to get back into a normal life. They assume it because they haven't been where you are and they don't know what they're talking about.

Say: "Actually, some days go very well and some days go very badly, and I think it will be quite a while before I'm really out of the woods."

6) **"Let me know if you need anything."**

Here's another generalization, an offer of help so vague that there's a real chance it's not genuine.

A dumpee who, between the time her husband walked and the time of their eventual financial settlement, was occasionally a few bucks away from eating catfood heard this remark several times from two friends, who also said, "Are you short for money?" One day, really broke, she asked one of those friends for a $200 loan. The friend said she was in a temporary bind herself and couldn't help. The dumpee was embarrassed.

When someone says, "Let me know if you need anything," reply: "I appreciate your saying that. At the moment I'm OK, but somewhere down the line I might really need some baby-sitting help [or a small loan or to borrow your car], and I'm glad to know I can call on you."

7) "Thank goodness you didn't have kids, so you don't have to have contact with the bum."

True, you need not go through the stressful business of arranging visiting days, turning your children over to the new woman on weekends, or hearing about her apple pie. But this reference to your childless state may stir up unhappy reflections that you're trying to avoid.

Says Laura: "Several people have said this to me, and I think, Yes, I am glad because I really don't want this man in my life anymore. On the other hand, when we were first together we used to talk about having kids. It was part of the picture I had of our life together. And I still would like to have a child at some point in time.

"I said that to a friend recently, and she said, 'You will.' And I thought, Or I may not—given my age, which my grandma likes to point out. She's actually saying to me now, 'Can't you just get pregnant and get married, or not necessarily get married, just get pregnant?'"

Reply to the "Isn't it good there are no kids" remark: "Yes, I know it would be more difficult now in some ways if children were involved. But I also feel regret about not having a child. So I have mixed emotions on that score."

There's Dead Silence from Some Formerly Friendly Corners

If some people make dumb remarks, others say nothing at all. Many dumpees report that after the split their crowd divided into the friends (usually women friends—the "girlfriends"; some men friends) and the couple friends. When you are no longer part of a couple, you often don't hear from the couple friends.

Later in this book we'll talk about your fractured social life and how to rebuild it. For now know that you may not be on everybody's "A" list for invitations anymore or that if you and your ex were part of a paired-off crowd, you may be left out of casual get-togethers, weekend plans, or other socializing you once enjoyed.

• • •

Going public as a new dumpee takes courage and stamina. You're over the worst part now.

3

Your Ex–Man

Out of Your Bed but Still in Your Life

After the first shock of betrayal has passed, after you've started to grow at least a thin film of scar tissue over the wound you suffered, you think about the kind of association you will or will not have with your ex. What that association will be has much to do with the circumstances of your particular dumping:

- Although until the end you saw each other exclusively, he lived in his place and you lived in yours. He had his car, his job, his furniture, and you had yours. Unentangled as you are financially and practically, if not yet emotionally, the break can be clean and swift—you need never see the guy again. But perhaps at some point you want to, for any one of a number of reasons we'll talk about later. Should you? If so, how?
- Although you had as yet no plans to marry, you lived together and in many respects *as if* married.

You bought a wall unit and sound system, half his money and half your money. You feel his absence in your life and home in an almost physical way. You've got to get his stuff—and possibly him himself—out of your place as well as your mind.

- You were dumped by your soon-to-be-ex-husband. You have children together. Maybe money and child visitation are not a huge problem, or maybe they are—the kids are confused, you're broke, an ugly court case seems likely. Many large issues and mundane details will need joint attention, and your association with your ex will necessarily be complex and ongoing.

Whatever your dumped scenario, you must make the moves that will be smartest in terms of your sanity, your happiness, and your future security. Even minimal contact with the man who left you can be a drain and a pain. Right now, you face some critical tasks:

> You must overcome any wish to go on the attack. Especially if you have a vested interest and/or share young children, civility—and good counsel—will help you get what you want and what your children need.

> You must keep beating back that urge to find out what's going on with him and your replacement.

> You must get his things out of your place. You must deal with sudden pangs of unhappi-

ness that come with living solo in a space you shared.

When, or if, you do talk to him about any of this, his comments may stun, enrage, or wound you.

Here we'll look at some steps you should take that will prevent you from making costly and humiliating mistakes as you maneuver your way through these difficult times.

Telephone Do's and Don'ts: Eight Smart Tips

If you have been following the *Dumped!* advice, you did not attempt to make contact with your ex during your walking wounded stage unless it was absolutely unavoidable for practical reasons. When you thought you couldn't stop yourself from dialing his number, you did stop, and you called a member of your support crew instead.

Now you do need to talk to him from time to time, probably to make arrangements concerning the dismantling of your joint life. Or, feeling stronger, you'd *like* to talk to him—to clear the air, get some questions answered, give him a piece of your mind.

Be careful. You're not as strong as you think, and hearing his voice may just stir up the pain and get you off the good track you're on. When you're thrown off track, you're liable to say things you will regret, and you'll definitely set back your forward progress in getting over him.

To establish safe and cordial phone contact with your ex:

1) Don't call him on the spur of the moment, on an impulse.

Plan a phone encounter ahead of time. You can't trust yourself to have a free-form conversation, even if all you want to do is say, "Hi, how are you?"

2) Don't call him in a snit.

One woman called her ex on his car phone, hopping mad after just learning that without consulting her he had dropped the asking price on their condo, which was up for sale. She instantly gathered from his hostile tone and stilted talk, she says, that his girlfriend was with him.

Phone calls when you're at the height of fury are a bad idea. You won't accomplish the call's purpose; you will just roil the waters some more.

3) Don't talk to him around midnight or after.

Another woman, several weeks after being dumped, called her ex at his apartment in the middle of the night. She said, "I'm not sleeping,

I'm sure you're not sleeping, do you want to talk?" He said he didn't, and she hung up angry and hurt.

Middle-of-the-night phone calls are a bad idea. If you're awake and roaming your place at 3 A.M. and think it makes sense to talk to the man who left you, you're still in a very negative state. The last thing you need is to hear his voice, probably with *her* as a witness.

If *he's* calling *you* regularly around midnight to discuss any business you need to settle, refuse to do so. He may be trying to jangle you by getting to you when you're tired and drained and not mentally sharp. Say: "I can't discuss this now, George, but I'll be happy to hear what you want to say tomorrow morning. I'll be here between ten and eleven. Good night."

4) **Don't call him at his new home.**

Do so only if your child is sick. Otherwise make any necessary calls to his place of work.

5) **If he has an office assistant, attempt to retain or establish good relations with this person.**

Say at the outset, "Jenny, I know this is awkward for us both, and I don't want to put you in an uncomfortable position. However, sometimes I will need to talk to George." Be polite. This person can be helpful to you in the coming weeks and months.

6)   When you must talk to him about practicalities, make an appointment to do so.

Don't, for example, call at nine in the morning and say, "I have to talk to George before nine-thirty." Say to Jenny or to George's answering machine: "I need to have a ten-minute conversation about three points. I'm available to do that either Tuesday morning or Wednesday between three and five." Then be available at that time.

7)   Make notes for yourself before and during the call.

If you and he are in negotiations about property, money, or children, write down what you want to say or find out. And surprise him by sticking to the established time frame. Say: "George, we've addressed only two of the items I needed to discuss with you, but our ten minutes are up. Do you want to continue now, or would you prefer to talk again tomorrow?"

A businesslike demeanor is the ticket here. It is in your own long-term best interests for him to realize that a call from you does not invariably degenerate into a harangue or a sob scene. Swear or sob after you get off the phone, if you must.

And make notes on what he says; a log may come in handy at a later date.

8) **If you're calling to suggest meeting for lunch or drinks, no hard feelings, no business, no heavy talk, just friends—stop and give yourself a little quiz.**

There may *be* a benefit in seeing your dumper again, even if it's not necessary—to reassure yourself that you're getting over him; to find out how he's doing; to notch up a little self-respect if during the dump you cried or raged or embarrassed yourself by trying to get him to stay; to put the anger behind you once and for all; to build confidence; to reestablish a friendship that meant a lot to you.

Before you can pull this off, you must be well and truly past your most vulnerable period. The last section of this chapter, "After the Dust Settles, Can You Be Friends?" provides some questions to ask yourself to determine if you can handle seeing him again—and tips on how to make the meeting a success.

Talking to Him: 13 Amazing Things Your Ex May Say to You and How to Respond

When you do talk or meet, and while he is perhaps still in a state of high romance with the new woman in his life, your ex-man will say things to you that boggle the mind. You will be amazed at his gall. You will be flabbergasted because it is utterly alien to what you would do if the tables were turned, if you were, say, running off with Mel Gibson. You'd have some compassion, not to mention couth, and you'd *never* rub his nose in it.

Sometimes you can prevent him from continuing. Sometimes you can attempt to correct his misperceptions. In any case, it helps to know what you might hear from your ex-man.

Dumpees report the following comments:

1) **"Barbie and I are probably going to get away to Hawaii for a few days."**

He sees nothing tacky in telling you about the new woman or plans he and she are making. Unless this information is relevant to your life, you do not want to hear it. If he starts to give you news about her, end it.

Say: "George, I'd prefer not to talk about Barbie." Then get the conversation back to the business at hand. It doesn't matter whether Barbie was just mugged or won the lottery; do not get dragged into discussing her at all, under any circumstances.

2) **"I really love her."**

When he's still all hot and heavy with the new woman, he may blurt out such remarks with no regard for the fact that he might as well peel your skin off.

Says Sheila: "We met several weeks before the divorce trial to try to work out a settlement, and toward the end of this conversation he told me he was so happy, he had really made the right decision, he loved Martha so much: 'I know you don't want to hear this, Sheila, but I really love her, I've learned so much about relationships and communication.' I sat there and thought, You jerk! Here you are sitting at a table with, technically, still your wife, and you're telling her how much you love another woman. What a cruel, insensitive bastard!"

Hurt and furious, she snapped at him: "I said, 'Well, Bill, if you've learned about relationships, good for you. Quite frankly, you have learned at my expense. And while I don't wish you ill health or any such misfortune, I *do* wish that one day Martha or someone else breaks your heart as deeply as you have broken mine.'"

Later she regretted that outburst. Her response sounded in her own ears immature and bitter.

If your ex starts rhapsodizing about the new love in his life, fight the temptation to remind him of the pain he has caused you. Even if you do stir up his guilty feelings, nothing has changed. Meanwhile, you are again fanning the flames of your own fury.

Do not let him continue his rhapsodizing, however. You do not have to listen to this. Say, simply and quietly: "George, no way. I will not discuss Barbie with you."

3) **"I never really loved you."**

This is worse than "I really love her." With this one he might as well drive an icepick through your heart.

Either he now so thoroughly views you as the enemy that he wants to hurt you some more, or he's settled on this explanation as a way to excuse his bad behavior (it was a big mistake in the first place, never meant to be, so of course I had to leave).

Say, in an amiable tone: "You know, I find that hard to believe. It sounds to me as if you're reconstructing history to suit your needs and make yourself feel better. In any case, I don't want to hear this from you now or get into any discussion of your feelings."

4) **"I never meant to hurt you."**

"I never meant to hurt you" is a line from a soap opera. Does it make a difference whether he meant to or didn't mean to? It doesn't.

Don't lash out in anger. At the same time, you don't have to let him off the hook with this mealy-mouthed attempt at self-justification.

Say: "The fact is, you have hurt me. You have hurt me badly. And that's a fact you must live with."

5) **"You never liked my friends."**

In other words, all this is really your fault.

If your ex is suggesting now, out of the blue, that things might have turned out differently if only you had tried harder to get along with his buddies or his mother, if you had shared his love of foreign movies, if you had not been so caught up in being promoted, you probably recognize a bald attempt on his part to shift the blame for the breakup to you.

Again, why let him off the hook? You can acknowledge an issue of conflict, if one existed, without accepting blame.

Say: "I'm sure you would have been happier if I hadn't had to put in such long hours at work, although you really didn't indicate to me that this was a huge problem in our relationship. In any case, it hardly justifies the way you went about ending the relationship. But let's not talk further about that now."

6) **"You've always been unresponsive."**

This is another, more hurtful it's-really-your-fault remark. Possibly sex was dropping off or nonexistent in the immediate predumped days. And now bad sex is what he holds against you.

Says one woman: "You know, I'm the obstacle, and he's actually come to hate me. He'll say anything to make himself not feel like the villain, and what he's been saying is that our sex life was lousy."

Don't get into this one. Say: "I have no intention of discussing which one of us was or was not sexually disappointing."

7) **"Barbie and I haven't had sex."**

The man who has not yet actually penetrated the new woman thinks you'll feel a lot better if he shares that fact with you. He doesn't understand that whether or not he has slept with her is not your primary concern.

As one dumpee says: "It's not the physical infidelity that bothers you as much as the betrayal of your relationship, the betrayal of intimacy. This man started conducting a life with someone else, when you thought you were his life. I don't care whether they've slept together or not."

You can try to explain this to your ex if you want to, but he won't get it. Better, say: "I really don't want to talk to you about Barbie, George."

8) **"I was, you know, involved with someone else before Barbie."**

The man who has just dumped you often feels a need to purge himself and will confess to matters that wound you anew. He will tell you that during the ten years you were together he was faithful for five.

If he starts to tell you about other affairs he's had, end it (unless you might find this information useful during divorce proceedings).

Say: "George, that's not important now." Or ask him to get tested for HIV or a sexually transmitted disease (see page 96).

9) **"There is no other woman."**

He is almost certainly lying through his teeth, but he is either too cowardly to fess up or he thinks he's helping you through the whole disaster gracefully. In fact, this assertion leaves you totally deflated—"There's no other woman, I don't have anyone else in my life, but I have to get rid of you, witch."

A dumper who announced he wasn't coming home anymore explained to his wife, "I just don't want to be married. I got married too young. It was a big mistake. I need to be on my own." She found out much later that at the time he had been carrying on a two-year affair, but before that discovery she reasoned with him: "I kept saying, 'Hey, look, fourteen years, two kids, it can't be over, let's go for counseling, let's take a vacation. Are you involved with another woman?' 'No, no,' he said. Finally I decided he might be gay."

There's no gain to challenging him on his there's-no-one-else assertion.

Say: "OK, fine."

10) "I knew you would be a survivor."

He thinks he's paying you a compliment.

Say: "Ooh, there you go underestimating me again, George. I've done a whole lot more than just survive." He'll wonder what you mean.

11) "I'll always take care of you."

This is nice, but don't bank on it. His generous intention may simply mean that at the moment he is feeling guilty, as well he should.

Say: "Well, good, George. And that's something we'll be discussing in more detail in the months ahead."

12) "We had some great times together, didn't we?"

Where in the dwindling days of your relationship he was hostile and distant, now he catches you off guard by suddenly acting pleasant, mellow, and eager for a trip down memory lane. He's no longer motivated to behave in those nasty ways, because he's achieved his aim, which—remember—was dumping you. Do *not* take such references to past pleasures as a sign that he's trying to patch things up or get back together.

If you're emotionally up for the memory lane trip, enjoy reminiscing. If you're not, say: "Yes, we did, but to tell you the truth it's painful for me to talk about that right now, so let's not."

13) "I enjoyed lunch, and I'm glad you suggested it, but I don't think we should do this again, OK?"

Ouch! You set up your let's-be-friends meeting, it went well, you were feeling *really* good that you could handle seeing him without a resurgence of all the old feelings or temptations. Now his unequivocal indication that he has no interest in a further association with you throws a damper on the moment. You'll get over it. Ideally, you've accomplished what you wanted to accomplish.

Give yourself a moment to regain whatever equilibrium you just lost. Then smile, nod, and say: "I'm glad we did this, too. It's been good seeing you."

Behind all these callous remarks, there is a stunning lack of caring about you and your feelings. It's been said that the opposite of love is not hate but indifference. As you find yourself talking to your ex-man in these early months, you may be amazed and appalled at how lightly his infidelity and betrayal sit on his shoulders. He acts as though it *just happened*—not that it required forward motion on his part. Be mentally prepared.

You, Your Ex, and the New Woman

Even if you are stoutly rebuffing any attempts he's making to share with you the good news about his new love life, you will find yourself wondering about her. Obsessing, in fact. What is she like? Why did he choose her over you?

Rein yourself in.

1) **Don't spy on them.**

The *occasional* dumpee has found that seeing the two of them together had a beneficial effect, sort of like putting a period at the end of the whole messy business.

Says Brenda: "I knew that Stan was taking his new girlfriend to the opening of a show at the museum, and I went specifically to see them. I spotted them, they didn't see me. I watched for a while, and then I left. I think before that it wasn't quite real to me that Stan and I were really over. It was torture, but seeing them together was a final push for me to let him go, give it up, and get on with my life."

For most women, however, searching out information on his new woman amounts to picking at the scab once again. It can delay your recovery and lead to unhealthy preoccupations.

For example, Susannah's rage at the man who dumped her was virulent. And yet: "On weekends, I would drive by the lot where he kept his car to see if the car was there or gone. When I knew he would be out of town on a business trip, I called his girlfriend's office and hung up when she answered. Why was I doing this? Why did I care? I didn't care. I was humiliating myself, and I couldn't stop myself."

If you're similarly drawn to keep tabs on your ex, you *must* stop yourself. Air these fixations with your support person or therapist. When you're tempted to put on a hat and shades, borrow someone's car, and loiter near his building to watch for comings and goings, get your support person to join you for a run around the high school track instead.

2) Don't call his girlfriend to tell her off, or send her pictures of you and your ex together in happier times.

Big mistake. You'll look like a fool. Besides, the truth is that even if the new woman was pushing your ex-man toward the dump, she didn't cause it. Another woman can derail a relationship; she can't end it. *He* can, and *he* did. It helps to remember that.

3) Try to avoid comparing yourself to her.

This is hard to do. What his new prize is like is part of the picture and part of how you will come to grips with it all in your mind. Even if you haven't seen or talked to her, you'll probably have learned something about her. That information tends to go one of two ways:

- Compared to you, she's a superior being.

One dumpee learned that her ex's girlfriend, a child psychologist, was having her Ph.D. thesis published and was a master cook, having studied at the Cordon Bleu in France. She was also gorgeous.

You will take such news and ponder it in your heart. Perhaps you will find that although the blow to your soul hurts no matter whom he dumped you for, the blow to your self-esteem is slightly less crushing if she's twenty years younger, a trial attorney, and looks great in jeans.

- Compared to you, she's an inferior being.

For Amelia, knowing quite a bit about the new woman only added to her sense of rejection because, she says: "This is no rocket scientist he's with now. So I have to get my head around the fact that here is a woman who says *sheepgoat* when she means *scapegoat* and whose idea of fun runs to pushing someone into the swimming pool. And my ex has said, 'I don't want you, I want her.' And I think, Wow! What is wrong with me that he went for *that*!"

Dumpee Alex's husband of ten years ran off with Polly and made her his new (third) wife. Says Alex: "We had both known Polly very casually for years because her son and ours were in the same class. And this is *not* an appealing person. Her language is crude. She's not attractive. Plus it is generally known that she'd fall into bed with anyone who was breathing. That this was the woman he left me for has been a bitter pill to swallow. Michelle Pfeiffer I could understand. But he dumped me for Polly. So what does that make me?"

If your scenario is similar, you may struggle with feelings that your own coinage as a woman has somehow been lessened by the choice he made. Work at overcoming all these ponderings. Comparisons will sap your emotional energy and distract you from moving on. They serve no good purpose.

4) Tell your ex what behavior you expect from him vis à vis her.

While it's generally best to know, hear, see, and talk about Barbie as little as possible, you are entitled to request that your ex follow certain ground rules pertaining to her. If you know that particular actions he might take with her would add to the emotional betrayal you've already suffered, ask him to refrain. He may, or he may not, but at least you have spoken your piece and made your feelings known.

One woman and her lover shared a small getaway house in the country, a place where they'd spent many happy hours. She says: "When the split came, I said to Paul, 'We'll have to decide about the house, and whoever ends up with it can do whatever he or she wants with it. But until then, you will not have Connie there, and I will not take another man there, because it's *our* house. While it's still our house, let's respect that.'

"I could almost imagine him having sex with this woman more readily than I could picture the two of them in that house together. It was terribly painful to think of her in the kitchen there, in the garden. He agreed. And then he didn't respect it. I found out from my neighbor in the country that he'd been up there having a party with Connie and her family."

Remember what we said: as he's moving into his new life, there's not a lot about his former one with you that he's going to hold sacred or off-limits. Tell him what you need or expect concerning his behavior with her on what is still your common ground, and hope he has the grace to honor any agreements you reach.

You are entitled, too, to ask for information that may have a bearing on your physical health. Says Kate: "I said to Rory, 'You've been having an affair with this woman over a period of time when you were also having sex with me. You told me she had an affair during that time with a married man. We have a lot of players here, and you've put my health at risk, so I want you to get tested.'"

Rory had a fit. What a bizarre suggestion, he said; he was fine, he had no intention of having any tests, he'd lose his health insurance, and on and on. Kate persevered. She made some phone calls, learned that his concerns about his insurance were unfounded, and faxed him a schedule of clinic hours.

Says another dumpee: "The week he left, I wrote a letter to my husband and said, 'Get tested for HIV. If you have a disease, I want to know about it.' He shouted at me over the phone. He said my letter was really vicious. 'Well,' I said, 'these are vicious times.'"

These were issues of real concern to the two women, and they insisted on satisfying those concerns. If you have reason for similar worries, you should get tested yourself.

Sometime in the future, although it's hard to believe right now, you may become, if not friends with the new woman, kindly disposed toward her. Sometime in the future you may even end up comparing war stories about the fellow you've shared; it's been known to happen.

Says one woman, whose children were four and six at the time of the dumping: "I had known Ellie, the one he moved in with and eventually married, for a long time. We had all worked for the same firm—I always did like her. Over the years—and this is now fifteen years after the fact—I found her easy to communicate with, easier than my ex-husband. She was very good to my kids, something that was most important to me. And lately she's been complaining to me about him!"

You may end up feeling quite grateful that *she's*

got him now, not you. As your hurt fades, you see this fellow as someone who maybe wasn't worth it for the long haul after all.

Or, if he left you for a twenty-five-years-younger woman, she may assume caretaking that you'll avoid, which can be a satisfying thought.

Fred, now eighty-four, left his wife Joan, now seventy-eight, two decades ago. Fred still loves to come by Joan's lovely house with its fragrant gardens on Sunday afternoons for some Bloody Marys, soup, and a chat. And at the end of their visit, Joan loves to help Fred back into his coat (he has mid-term Alzheimer's now) and point him down the road toward his own home.

She says: "I'd feel sad if he went off and wasn't looked after. And I'm *very* happy that she took him on and has the responsibility. I wouldn't like it if he'd run off with a silly girl. He was a good man, just stupid about women."

His Stuff, Your Stuff: The Mechanics of Separation and Removal

Most dumpees don't report a lot of hassles over who gets what household objects. Unless there are items of personal interest or big value at stake, it's unlikely that your ex will dicker with you now over things you have both lived with.

Most men are like birds who move to another's nest with ease; they usually don't require the accoutrements of the old homestead. Also, his feelings of guilt over dumping you, flickering though they may be, will prevent him from asking for the sofa. (That may come later.) And then, of course, all that stuff represents the life he wanted out of.

Dealing with "stuff" is going to be harder for you, emotionally invested as we women tend to be in the places we call home. Here are five steps to make separating possessions easy on yourself:

1) Set up a specific time for him to come by to collect his things, and don't be there when he does.

If you've been living together, presumably he'll want to pick up clothes and personal items. It will be better for you if you're elsewhere because watching him pack up his shirts, softball mitt, and *MAD* magazine collection may strike you like a stab in the heart or a red flag to a bull.

Better than letting him do the packing, throw all those items into cartons before the appointed pickup so they're ready to go. You'll be more thorough than he, and you won't run the risk two weeks later of coming upon his old sweatshirt overlooked on a hook in the closet, which will make you feel weepy.

2) Go see a mindless movie with your support person while the pickup is going on, and have her

come back to your place with you afterward for a simple dinner or cheese and wine. It may be painful to walk back into the place you shared with your ex and face the evidence that he's removed the last vestiges of his presence there.

One dumpee's husband had a large personal collection of antique wall clocks, which he took from their apartment, as arranged, one day while she was at work. Coming in her door that evening, the sight of her bare walls was like a punch in the stomach: "We'd hung those clocks in the entry hallway. They were a focal point of the apartment, a big conversation piece, something I'd lived with and enjoyed for years. To come in and see them gone was shocking. I felt like I'd been robbed."

Even if the stuff your ex removed was confined to a couple of drawers and a shelf in the bathroom, you may feel sad at first to see those empty spaces. This is a good time to have a friend around.

3) If he drags his feet about the pickup, send his things to him.

If he refuses to collect his stuff or just isn't getting around to doing it, you'll have to take care of this business yourself. One bonus of being dumped is a freeing up of closet space, and you shouldn't have to delay that pleasure because of his dawdling or carelessness. Also, you may be tempted to think that as long as his possessions are still in your place, he's not really gone from your life, a line of thought that is counter-productive to your forward progress.

4) Give or throw his things away.

Getting his possessions to him isn't a huge problem if it's a matter of clothes or personal items that can easily be stuffed into a couple of plastic trash bags or cartons from the liquor store and brought or delivered to wherever he's living at the moment. It *is* a problem if you're looking at bigger, heavier, unwieldy stuff. Don't bend yourself out of shape or go to great expense to rid your home of his odds and ends.

Give him fair warning and a time limit; then donate it all to a local thrift shop.

5) Try to divide jointly purchased or jointly received items equitably—and *early*.

As we've said, your ex is probably not making demands for household possessions at this point. Says one woman: "I asked him to come over and look around and write out a list of what he wanted. He said, 'I don't care. I don't know what we have.' Finally he did come over, and I went out for the afternoon. When I returned he was gone, but there was no list. I called, and he said he just played with the cat and left."

Sounds good—but what you *don't* want happening is a request from him some months or years later (when he's feeling less guilty or setting up a new apartment) for the Bokhara in the living room or the dining room table. You don't want that happening because it will disrupt your life all over again, make you angry, and easily provoke a fight.

So make your own list of stuff you bought together, and insist he spend some time working out with you a sensible distribution. Strive to be fair. Don't get into unnecessary squabbles over things you can replace or live without.

Perhaps you will need to get *him* out of there.

It doesn't happen often, but a few women we've talked to report that after the dumping, their men refused to move out. In two cases, money—a whole lot of it or not enough of it—was the issue.

Renee's husband told her he was involved with someone else, their marriage was dead, and he thought it would be a good idea if she vacated their elegant co-op—within two weeks. Says Renee: "Wally's mother's money, it's true, is largely what financed us for this place years ago. But he's the one who wanted out. He should *get* out, literally."

Renee and her soon-to-be-ex cohabitated for months until everybody went to court. Since the place had fourteen rooms, divided into two wings, she was able to maintain this sticky arrangement without actually bumping into him too often.

Ellen's boyfriend became involved with a flight attendant based in Miami, on the other side of the continent. It was soon clear to Ellen that he had no immediate plans to relocate; he also had next to no money. So, she says: "I couldn't get him out of my apartment! He just refused to move. He and his dog stayed in one bedroom, I stayed in the other."

You *must* get him out, as expediently as possible! When money, jointly owned or jointly deeded property, and divorce are involved, talk to your lawyer. Otherwise, change the locks.

Alone in Your Old Home

Once he and his stuff are out of there, you'll look around and see your new old home. It's the same, and it's not.

Some dumpees feel an instinct to flee, to move on to a new place that signifies the start of a new life. Says one who did that: "If you're fairly secure and up for change, which I was, and young children are not in your life and money is not a major issue, I recommend it highly. Getting a new apartment gave me a huge emotional charge, one that carried over into all areas of my life."

Most stay put, either because selling and moving are not financially feasible or wise, or because children need the security of a place they know during a time of upheaval, or because the woman herself finds comfort there. One dumpee says that leaving her office and returning to her old familiar apartment on her lunch break each day was what kept her going in the beginning; she felt safe there.

If you're struggling through your most wounded phase in the place you once lived in together while he has moved on to another place, expect some melancholy times. There will be much to sweep you back again and again to earlier, sweeter days—those place mats, that CD you liked to play on Sunday mornings, the jumbo-sized jar of Dijon mustard that he used to make his vinaigrette. You open a cabinet or drawer, and suddenly something in there reminds you of a fun evening you had, friends who came over. You feel sad again.

Those kinds of gloomy thoughts won't go on forever, even if you remain in your old place. In the meantime, try to make it more yours and less "ours," as far as the budget will permit. Maybe it won't involve any budget at all. The dumpee who moved immediately to "his" side of the queen-sized bed realized after a week or two that she'd never liked the bed against that wall in the first place. She pushed it into the middle of the room, still sleeps on his side, and says she loves getting into *her* bed at night.

Give away the Sunday morning CD—get a new one.

Throw out the mustard—develop a new salad dressing.

Make as many no-cost decorative changes as you can. Just rearranging furniture a little will give your living room a new post-ex look and feel.

Invest some money, as much as you can afford, in reinventing those two most intimate areas, the bedroom and the bathroom. Don't even wait for the sales; go out and charge a new set of sheets and new towels. If you had all white before because that's what he preferred, go for a pastel print or purple with embroidery. Sleep on and dry off with virgin cloth.

This is now *your* place, so make it you.

Your Lawyer, Your Mouthpiece

As we've said, this book is not about divorce, it's about women getting dumped. That being resaid, we add: Divorce, of course, is commonly the final step in the process for married dumpees. And divorce is essentially a business deal.

Much of the contact you'll have with your ex-man in the weeks, months, even year or more after he has walked will concern the business deal—who gets what. Occasionally a dumper is zapped out of nowhere with love for a new woman; he's compelled to follow his heart and go off with her with no more than the shirt on his back. He wishes you well and gives you everything, every last cent. You probably don't have one of those.

Here is the typical, woefully common scenario: By the time your husband announced to you that he was moving on, he'd been contemplating the act for a long time. Not only contemplating it—planning it. He's lined up both the new woman *and* the new life. Perhaps he's already taken measures to use, cash in, or move assets in ways that will enable him to leave you with as few of them as possible.

While you are still staggered by the betrayal, he is way, way ahead of you. While you are still forcing yourself to change out of your pajamas in the morning and wondering how to tell your mother, he is putting the final touches on the "settlement package" he intends to present to you. You're reeling emotionally; he's ready to do business.

As stated earlier, he has a dazzling capacity to compartmentalize his life. Whatever guilt or dismay he feels about shattering you does not prevent him from going crisply off to work, handling the merger or running the auto parts shop or doing whatever it is he does. You, on the other hand, are like a sieve— you need all your energies just to stop the anger, unhappiness, and anxiety about being dumped from seeping into every activity and moment of the day.

He's geared to move forward. You're still trying to figure out what hit you. Given that picture, you are inevitably reacting to him and to a timetable he has set. You're vulnerable to being pressured into making quick decisions and "getting it all over with" at a time when you're least likely to think logically. Here's where the good counsel comes in.

Right at the start, you sought out a lawyer for an exploratory meeting or two, and you should have an idea whether or not this individual will do the job you need done. What that job is depends to a large degree on what you know about your ex-man.

Says Christine: "My husband actually warned me. He said, 'If you get a shark on me, I'll take everything off shore.' I knew that if I came in with some real tough nut of a lawyer, Frank would wipe the floor with me."

It's a not uncommon attitude among rich, successful men. One well-known multimillionaire was asked if he intended to give more than had been agreed upon before the marriage to his recently dumped second wife, who was voicing her discontent and spending a lot of time in her lawyer's office. The dumper was quoted as replying, "I would say that if she challenges the prenuptial agreement, the answer is no. If she doesn't challenge it, the answer is possibly."

So a lawyer who's ready to move in the big guns after you've talked to him or her for half an hour may not serve you well.

Says one woman: "The first lawyer I consulted said, 'Let's take this guy to the cleaners.' He was smelling blood. And I said I was not going to do that to my husband. It didn't feel right—and it was too soon to be drawing up a whole attack plan. Besides, my thought at that moment was, my husband's best asset is his ability to earn, and I can alienate him very quickly with the wrong moves."

On the other hand, maybe a shark *is* right for you.

Says Jane: "I got a lawyer who could have been cast as a hit man. And Brad, my husband, had a killer. These two lawyers spoke the same language, and I think that's when Brad realized I was deadly serious."

Analyze your ex and find the lawyer you need. If you suspect you haven't got the right man or woman for the job, ask around some more. Network like crazy. Talk to your friends, and ask them to talk to their friends, and soon you will come up with a short list of lawyers.

At the same time, inform yourself. Buy a divorce workbook. Call your local bar association and request a copy of the divorce code. Get as much information about your husband's assets as you can. Says one dumpee: "I say to other women, as soon as you read the handwriting on the wall, start looking after yourself and start acting like a man would act, which is basically—cover your ass."

Then, work with what you've learned and with the lawyer you've picked. You may need this individual to help you decide whether it is in your best interests to prolong settlement negotiations or to move quickly (a few dumpees have found that right after the split the ex is likely to ante up the most—when the other woman moves more fully into the picture, he's going to offer less and drag it out); how to handle any threats he is making concerning custody; how to proceed if *he* is making noises about suing *you* for support. Your lawyer may also be able to tell you how much money you can reasonably expect in settlement (in many states, this is almost a formula).

Prepare yourself for your lawyer meetings. Says one woman: "Arm yourself with a specific list of questions. Don't think of the lawyer as some sort of counselor. Remember that the lawyer will be perfectly happy to keep handing you tissues as you sob about the cad you married, but every tissue will cost you more than you imagine. Save the tears for your support group."

What the right lawyer can do for you, at the very least, is reinforce the reality that you're conducting a business deal, and that's a reality that many women don't grasp.

You can be mad as hell and determined to get what you deserve and *still* lose heart or feel queasy about the prospect of fighting for it. That's when a supportive lawyer can shore up your resolve and keep you focused.

Dana resisted the suggestion of issuing a court order to her husband because, she says: "I didn't want to embarrass him. I was protecting him. And in the back of my mind was the thought that all this will become public and it will somehow seem like my fault. So for months I was telling myself, I'll just see how Peter plays this out, and if he's decent I'll toe the party line. Then I heard that he was telling people at work and in our social circle *his* story, which was lies, and my lawyer said, 'Enough is enough, time to wake up.' And I thought, That's it—the gloves are off." She proceeded to take legal action.

Vanessa and her ex-lover, Zack, ended up going to court to decide the fate of some property they owned. "My lawyer gave me some excellent advice," she says. "He said, 'You have only one chance. So don't think about Zack's feelings. A woman has a problem. She's been thinking about the man's feelings for years. She's accustomed to worrying about what's good for the *guy*. Then when it comes down to fighting for herself, she's afraid of hurting him or looking like a bitch. Don't think that way!'

"That was very helpful advice. Because it's

true—even though you've been betrayed, you're still nurturing. That's the woman's way. The lawyer said, 'Go in there like a pit bull. Look like a lawyer, talk like a lawyer, and get what you deserve.'

"We went to court, and I was prepared. I was organized. I was wearing a power suit! Afterward, Zack said to me, 'You were really something in there, I admired you.'"

More often, according to many women, the tough, in-charge stance rouses the ex-husband's ire. Says one dumpee: "A huge problem I've had is defending the fact that I hired a lawyer who showed me how to get information. I learned that my soon-to-be-ex had money I didn't know anything about. But he's giving me a lot of heat and telling everyone I'm just stalling and running up his bills."

Or he may try to persuade you that by getting a lawyer you're just wasting money, that you and he can handle everything—in fact, *he'll* handle everything. One dumper told his wife, "We want to stay friends, don't we? Don't waste all this money on lawyers. I'm going to be completely fair."

Don't count on it.

And although it will hurt, realize that at this point you are a business deal to your ex.

Getting Even: A Little Revenge for the Soul

When Marjorie's dumper returned their daughter on a Sunday evening after a weekend in which he and his woman friend had treated the girl to an amusement park outing, Marjorie followed her ex out to the elevator. They exchanged a few unpleasantries regarding the next week's pick-up and drop-off arrangements. The elevator was right beside a flight of stairs.

Says Marjorie: "He stood waiting for the elevator with that smug look on his face, and I had a sudden urge to push him down the stairs. I could easily have done it. I really don't know how I managed not to."

If your ex is making hurtful remarks or looking at you with indifference, you may be feeling a similar almost uncontrollable urge to harm him. It's not uncommon. Dumpees have been known to retaliate in some terrible ways.

There was the California woman who went to the home of her ex-husband and his new love, found them in bed, and shot them dead. There was the Vancouver mother of six who cut off her husband's penis and flushed it down the toilet (one presumes to eliminate any possibility of surgical reattachment).

Then there was the dumped girlfriend who, upon moving out, stuffed baby shrimp into the curtain rods, and the woman who cut the crotches out of all her husband's designer suits.

Certainly you don't wish to go so far as to kill or maim or to do anything nasty with rotting fish or scissors. However, neither are you in a mood to turn the other cheek and let bygones be bygones. So how do you get some satisfaction?

You've heard that living well is the best

revenge, which is certainly true—and you *will* get to the living well part with determination and a measure of luck. While you're toying with baser thoughts, however, remember the difference between bad revenge and good revenge—or dumb revenge and smart revenge.

Dumb revenge is any action that is:

1) Personally degrading or embarrassing or will make you come across as a bitter, possibly unhinged woman.

Saying mean things or spreading distasteful rumors about your ex's new woman, for example, makes you look like a bitch. It's perfectly all right if your *friends* want to spread rotten stories about her, but you shouldn't.

2) Unlawful and may cause a policeman to stop by your door one evening for a chat.

Taking a key to your guy's cherished BMW and creating some gouges, for example, can leave you open to charges of vandalism and criminal mischief. Cutting the arms off all his jackets can be considered defacing personal property. It's unlikely he would try to have you arrested, but why take a chance?

3) Obsessive or subconscious.

If you keep wanting to get back at him and can't redirect your energies, you'll never move on to your new life. If you keep taking revenge in small passive-aggressive ways, like never having your children packed and ready when he comes to pick them up for the weekend, you're not moving on and you're hurting people you love.

Smart revenge is taking an appropriate action that leaves you feeling better. You can:

1) Have your day in court.

If you're a married dumpee and galled at no-fault divorce because you think there damn well should be some fault, file for divorce on the grounds of adultery. Says one woman: "I thought, If I have to go through this, I will get some small satisfaction by calling him an adulterer, which of course he was and is."

If you happen to live in one of the several states that still carry two-hundred-year-old alienation of affection laws, you might want to consider suing the new woman for homewrecking. A North Carolina jury awarded one dumpee a million dollars, to be paid by her ex-husband's new wife. Although the dumpee doesn't expect to collect much or any of this, she feels quite pleased with the court action.

2) Cause him to spend a lot of money.

It's satisfying, says one woman, to watch him go into hock to a bunch of lawyers: "I didn't receive much in the way of financial gains, but I knew what his legal fees were, and they were astronomical."

Another woman, ticked off at the sight of her ex's clothes taking up space in her apartment, got revenge by shipping them to the cleaners: "I paid a kid in my building to pack up all the stuff and take it over to the dry cleaners. Everything—jackets, sweatclothes, pants, shirts, ties, underwear, handkerchiefs. I had the underwear starched and pressed. I had everything delivered to him at his new place, with the bill, of course."

3) Enjoy watching people turn their backs on him.

While it certainly doesn't always happen, some dumpers find themselves the target of a great deal of ill feeling from former friends. Says one woman: "We had a lot of friends, people we both enjoyed. I was the one who kept these friendships going. After he left me, because his behavior was so reprehensible, most of our mutual friends were appalled and didn't want to have anything to do with him. He lost everyone from that crowd."

4) Stick pins in his picture.

Delia's young-adult children presented her at Christmas with a dartboard that had a blown-up photo of her husband's face in the center. The dartboard remained in a prominent place for all to see and was much in use over the holidays.

Linda chanced upon a fantastic low-priced two-week cruise in the South Pacific with a friend whose mother had to back out at the last minute. Persuaded by her boss to take the time and blow the money, Linda felt madly extravagent and blissfully free. She took with her a fat envelope full of photos of herself and her ex-boyfriend at holiday gatherings and on vacations: "Midway through the cruise, I took all these photos one night, sat by myself at the stern, and threw them overboard. After all, they're biodegradable."

5) **Know that he'll probably die before his time.**

According to several scientifically conducted surveys, married dumpers are looking at a bumpy road ahead. Men who get divorced are more likely than nondivorced guys to go into psychiatric hospitals and to die prematurely of heart disease, pneumonia, or suicide. This *may* offer you some comfort, but as we noted earlier, this usually happens to other women's ex-husbands.

6) **Know that before long the new woman will probably start seeming old hat.**

For some dumpers, moving on is a matter of change partners and dance. Nothing much is different except that she's a new face—maybe the first of several. Will he be happy? Possibly, possibly not.

Says Allegra: "I still talk to Phil off and on, and from what he says there's no question in my mind that the passion between the two of them has worn off. He once said to me, 'I've been happy with any woman I've ever dated—it's just that I get caught up in getting something new.' The newness for him with Debra is gone. He might just as well have stayed with me—the relationship with her is probably the same now as it was between us at the end."

It doesn't make you a bad person if you take some pleasure in contemplating and enjoying this scenario. His new woman may very well have the same experiences with him that you had, especially if this guy has a history of playing around. If he had problems in your relationship, and he was unwilling or unable to address them, they're likely to resurface. The new woman is just another aspect of the ongoing difficulties he has in sharing his life with another person, or in being honest, or in making commitments. He'll repeat old patterns.

If in the first blush of love he sent you forty dozen yellow roses, Barbie probably got her roses too. If after the blush was gone he told you on New Year's Eve that he was leaving, Barbie may get similar news a New Year's Eve or two from now. These fellows are nothing if not creatures of habit.

Says Eleanor: "He's had a series of younger women. Oddly, I think my main view of him now is that I feel sorry for him. He doesn't seem very happy, while I feel quite content."

What goes around comes around—not always but sometimes. Or as Shakespeare wrote, "the whirligig of time brings in his revenges." At any rate, you're focusing on moving on with your own life, regardless of what life holds in store for him.

After the Dust Settles: Can You Be Friends?

The majority of dumpees we've talked to seem to consider the notion of an ongoing chummy relationship with the ex-man unappealing. If *he's* suggesting any such thing, they find it bizarre.

Says one woman: "He tried, pretty actively for the first year or so, to be friends. His idea seemed to be that I'd find someone new and the four of us could double-date. That is just a little too Hollywood for me! Finally I had to say to him that I didn't think it was normal, and I couldn't imagine having a friendly relationship with someone who had done to me what he did."

Another ex, who moved to a different state, calls the woman he dumped when he comes to town on business, leaving messages on her answering machine that they might meet for a drink or take in a concert together. She says: "He thinks we should be friends. I can't imagine anything more scary. Why would I want this odious person in my life?"

The occasional dumpee, however, sees the possibility of friendship with her ex. Says one: "I was with Barry for a long time. And I don't understand why, if you loved somebody enough once to live with him and sleep with him, you wouldn't want that person as a friend for life. I'd like to have that with Barry now, but the woman he left me for—who's now his wife—won't let it happen. She's not comfortable with the idea. I talked to him about all this a while ago, and I said, 'Excuse me, I never tried to steal you from her, why is *she* uncomfortable?'

"In fact, he and I now have a friendly, secret relationship on the phone—we talk during the day, mostly about our work. His wife doesn't know. He wants that relationship with me. He likes me. And really, I like him."

For another woman, a married dumpee who went through a particularly painful divorce, reestablishing a cordial connection with her ex much later was a conscious step in her own healing: "I decided all this staying angry on my part wasn't good for anybody—not for the children, not for him since it just made him feel worse, and definitely not for me. It was diminishing me. I made the decision not to be angry anymore, and that has really helped me in my mind. I forced myself to say, 'This is bad, stop the anger!' And I arranged to meet him. Now I can be around him. We have lunch from time to time and talk, small talk really, and it's been fine. I think I'm just kind of slowly moving away from him. He's fading away."

Perhaps you are wondering now if there's any point to connecting again with the man who walked. Perhaps you had no practical or family issues to see or talk to him about, you've had no contact with him since he left, and—for any of the reasons we mentioned at the beginning of this chapter—you're thinking of giving him a call and suggesting you meet.

Before plunging ahead, ask yourself these questions:

Has it been less than six months since you were dumped?

Are you still having walking wounded attacks, days you have a really hard time going about your life?

Are you having trouble eating wisely?

Do you sometimes still fantasize about what it would be like if you got back together?

Do you conduct conversations with him in your mind?

When you go to a party or out with friends, do you find as the evening goes on that you can't enjoy yourself?

Do you want to ask your ex why he *really* left?

When you thought you spotted him walking across the street, did your heart jump and your pulse pound?

Does he pop into your mind whenever the phone rings?

Since you decided to call him, have you become desperate to see him again?

If you're coming up with yes answers, forget about attempting a friendly encounter right now—you won't be able to manage it. Worse, you'll reopen the wound and possibly behave in ways that will humiliate you.

Act on your instinct to get in touch with him *only* if you are well past the worst of the hurt (and remember, that may take months or years), well launched into your new life, and ideally have found someone else to like (if not love) and have some fun with. If you're at that happy place, still proceed with caution:

1) Plan the phone call before you make it, including the place you will suggest meeting, which should *not* be your apartment or any restaurant you two frequented in your couple days. Brunch or lunch is good; drinks after work is not good.

Sound cheerful and upbeat, and don't in words or tone give the impression that you want to rehash the old business. Although that's probably what he *will* think, it must not be what you intend or want. Don't make any reference to "for old time's sake." After the hello's and how-are-you's, say: "I'd enjoy seeing you again, and I wonder if you're free for lunch some day this week or next."

If he says no or "Uh, well, I don't know if that's such a hot idea," say: "OK. I'm still at the same place. Give me a call if you're free or change your mind."

If he doesn't, don't try again.

2) If he's agreeable, tell him where and when to meet, and end the conversation right away.

3) On the day, look good; do *not* look as if you're out to knock his socks off with your gorgeousness.

If you're spending more than fifteen minutes figuring out what you'll wear, this whole idea may be a big mistake and you're not ready after all. Too late now, so just get a grip on yourself, dress attractively, and don't wear his favorite outfit or anything he gave you as a gift. You may hope to make him reflect on what a fool he was to let you go, but don't allow yourself to entertain such thoughts for very long.

4) Before you leave for your meeting, imagine what you might hear from the guy.

Review "Talking to Him: 13 Amazing Things Your Ex May Say to You and How to Respond," earlier in this chapter. Be prepared.

5) Stick to neutral conversation. Talk about work, his family, your family, mutual friends.

6) **Keep the get-together short.**

Your lunch or brunch should last one hour, one-and-a-half hours tops. At that time, say you must get back to work, and call for the check. You pay.

7) **Say, "I'd like it if we kept in touch," if that's how you feel. Leave separately.**

To be or not to be friends with your ex is a highly personal decision. Make the effort if you're so motivated and if, after rigorous self-assessment, you decide you're ready.

•   •   •

Getting your dumper out of your life should be easy—since, after all, he left. Often, however, it takes determination, work, and a marked degree of self-awareness. It helps to remember that.

What Did I Do Wrong?
How Could I Have Been So Stupid?
(Can I Get Him Back?)

A Self-Esteem Restoration Plan

It's possible that being dumped has not affected your self-esteem. Maybe you have no concerns that it might be something about your face, figure, intelligence, sexuality, housekeeping skills, or sense of humor that caused your guy to flee. While you *may* be this self-assured, it's not bloody likely!

Chances are that like the vast majority of dumpees, you're spending at least part of the time trying to figure out just where you were at fault. If your ex was contemplating his actions for a while, he may have deliberately or unconsciously planted small seeds of doubt about your worthiness as a girlfriend or wife. If you bought into this, it would assist him in assuming the role of disappointed mate for you to be cast as the one who was sadly lacking.

Now that you're getting out of the walking wounded stage, it's time to look at all this with as cold an eye as you can muster. You've *got* to get past the fact that this is a guy who once found you adorable and thought you walked on water. These days he considers you a barrier to his happiness with someone else.

"No matter how you look at it," says one dumpee, "no matter if you *know* in your heart of hearts that you are one hell of a great woman, the fact is, he left you. That's the foundation of the hurt, a knife blade in the very core of your self-esteem. So you start thinking, well, maybe I wasn't so great after all."

Wondering about your part in the demise of the relationship is not only par for the course; it can be a cathartic endeavor and a sound step on the road out of the past and into your future. Better to face your self-doubts head-on than to continue feeling vaguely on the defensive or, worse, as if you triggered the whole collapse.

Examine it and then put it behind you. You *don't* want to be grappling with what-if's for years. This apparently is the case with a prominent political candidate's first wife, dumped more than two decades ago, who said in an interview just before the last election: "It's always been a mystery to me why it happened. I could have been just as much to blame for the problem as he was. That was my biggest question: What did I do wrong?"

Ask it now, take a clear-sighted accounting, draw your conclusions, and then stop second-guessing your former life. One woman calls this "running down the deficiency list: What didn't I do enough of? What did I do too much of? What was I not?"

Herewith, according to dumpees interviewed, are the ten most common what-did-I-do-wrong questions along with new, better questions to ask yourself.

1) **"Did I pay enough attention to him?"**

Alice, an accessories buyer for a fashion designer, claims to have "zero interest" in sports. Her ex-boyfriend, Jake, a stock analyst, enjoyed boating and other outdoor activities. Early on, Alice went on several sailing expeditions, which she found a bore; thereafter she was content to let Jake go off with his outdoorsy buddies while she focused on work. She remembers that she once took a two-week buying trip to Japan and China over Thanksgiving, "and the Thanksgiving holiday was always very important to him."

Jake dumped her for a woman who loved boats and hiking. Now Alice wonders if her ex felt "abandoned" by her a lot of the time.

Lucy says that over the years, she and her husband started "living in parallel universes," and she thinks she should have tried harder to spend more time in his—or at least to notice more what was going on there.

She says: "He worked long hours. During all those years I was having a good time with the children, I was caught up in their school activities, had many friends, and did a lot of volunteer work. He had his things, I had my things.

"His company got season box seats to various games, and there were always other company events and activities going on. It was a hassle for me to get to these affairs because I had to arrange baby-sitting and so on. He'd tell me he was going with people from his office, which turned out to be mainly his secretary. But I'm not a tight-rein person, and I wasn't about to worry about his socializing."

Now, she says, "that's how I let the marriage stray off track."

- A new, better question: "Did he pay attention to me?"

If you believe you should have been more attentive to his needs and wishes, consider whether your ex paid enough attention to yours.

Alice stopped thinking she had "abandoned" Jake; although she didn't share some of his interests, she knows she was a loving companion in most ways. Besides, she says: "He knew that my job was as important to me as his job was to him. Sometimes I *had* to be out of town on business. He needed to understand that, and *I* need to not blame myself for it."

Lucy's former husband, especially in the immediate predump months, left the house at 6:30 A.M. and returned at midnight, day after day. "I used to kid him," she says, "that I never got out of my bathrobe all day, because that was the only thing he ever saw me in." Although "he had his things, I had my things," she hadn't been happy for a long time: "We had a boat, a ski cabin, all the trappings, but it was not my idea of success. The kids never saw him, I never saw him. This was our marriage. It didn't start out that way, but it seemed to end up that way. It got so he really knew very little about me and what my days were like."

She also remembers that she tried to change the picture. She talked to him about her need for more of him, she told him how hard it was to get herself to the after-work activities. "We had four children, after all," she says.

Several years after he dumped her, Lucy realized that her ex was repeating his same old patterns with his new wife—little time for the children, sixteen-hour days, a wife who seemed largely left to her own amusements. She says: "My kids used to come back from staying with them and say, 'Mom, Dad hasn't changed, that's just the way he is.' It was important for me to understand that I hadn't made him that way."

Reflect on the quality of your days together, what you gave and what you got back. Perhaps, like many dumpees, you will analyze the quid pro quo in your relationship and see clearly that he made few efforts to accommodate you.

2) **"Was I no good in bed?"**

One way your ex may be pushing your buttons right now is by veiled—or not so veiled—references to your sexual chilliness, your lack of imagination in bed. This, of course, is a killer item on anybody's deficiency list because it strikes at the core of your womanhood. And it implies that now, at last, he's finally found a "real" woman.

Says Marjorie: "From some comments he made to me during the last months we were together and some remarks since he left, I get the impression I was supposed to be Demi Moore doing a striptease or Elizabeth Berkley with the pole number. Or I should have been doing cartwheels in bed or tried it on a trampoline."

- A new, better question: "How could we have good sex when he was preparing to dump me?"

Your unsatisfactory sex probably did not start out that way. Marjorie remembers: "Sex was good with us in the beginning, fair to lousy to nothing at all for the last year. It's true I wasn't in a mood to get the flame going again. But, of course, neither was he. He had emotionally withdrawn so much, sex was almost out of the question." In any case, she adds: "I didn't go looking for somebody new."

You probably didn't either. If you had for some time been unhappy with the love-making between the two of you, chances are you tried to make it better by suggesting joint counseling, or by taking *yourself* to a therapist, or by picking up a magazine that promised to tell you ten ways to put the zing back in your sex life. You didn't go looking for a new man.

Says one woman: "Nothing is all one-sided, and certainly I had something to do with the break-down of our sex life. But I was loyal. Most women are loyal. Men, on the other hand—you'd think they could stay celibate when they have to be out of town for ten days."

Don't berate yourself now as a lousy lover. Good sex for a woman requires a good atmosphere—of love, affection, and trust, and that you didn't have.

3) "Did I put all my energies into being a mother, not enough into being a wife?"

Helen says she thinks her story is not uncommon: "I was married at twenty, right out of college. Where I came from, you *went* to college to find a husband, and I was married for thirty-five years, had three children. I think for a lot of the women of my generation, the children became somewhat consuming. The man was gone a lot of the time, the woman 'did' the kids and the house. I'm sure my ex-husband would say now that I was a wonderful mother but not much of a wife."

- A new, better question: "Was he much of a father?"

If you're concerned that you were overly consumed with the children, was it because he was "underly" so?

Janice says she and her son and daughter "became a world unto ourselves": "I know what role a father should play because it was one my dad had with my sister and me. He was very busy with his business, but he was also extremely close to us, and we felt that. I think my husband, on the other hand, had rather a hard adjustment to being a father. When he wasn't at work, he found it easier to get involved with the golf course than with his children. The kids were missing out on so much. I know I was compensating for what they didn't get from him."

Says another dumpee: "My husband, like most men these days, expected superwoman. I always had a job and made money, I had the babies, I raised the kids, I went to the parent-teacher meetings and the swimming lessons and the birthday parties. He, meanwhile, was the white knight who breezed in, had dinner, maybe played a little game of Candyland with them, and then went to read the papers and watch TV. Mom is on deck for everything—Dad does the special stuff, and only when he feels like it."

One of you had to be the full-time parent. Probably that role fell to you at least in part through default.

4) **"Was I too wishy-washy and dependent?"**

Adrienne says: "The relationship had not been perfect by any means, and in all fairness to my husband I have to say that he was aggressive and successful and loved life and had a lot of energy. He was a strong personality, and he really was responsible for most of the momentum in our life. It was hard to create momentum on my own merits—he just could do it better!

"He had various women, over time, and I lost self-respect, to the point where he finally won, he pushed me over the edge. His comment to me when he left was that I had become a doormat. But there just didn't seem to be the opportunity in that marriage for me to be independent."

- A new, better question: "What were my strengths?"

If, like Adrienne, you lived with an overbearing powerhouse of a man, you may have felt like the lesser partner. Now that you're out of his shadow, it's time to look at yourself in the full light of day.

Make up a sufficiency list to go along with your deficiency list. Spend an hour with your journal and write down all the things you did as a lover, wife, or mother that you did reliably, adequately, or perhaps splendidly well. Get beyond all-or-nothing thinking. You had your shortcomings, but a few shortcomings do not a door-mat make.

5) **"Did I focus on his flaws and overlook his virtues?"**

Maybe your ex has sterling qualities—he's affectionate to old people, kids, and pets, he's loyal to his friends, he's fun at a party. Aside from his unkind dumping of you, you think he's pretty decent. *Other people* think he's pretty decent and are telling you so. You wonder if you were always too critical of him or if you compelled him to find applause for those sterling qualities elsewhere.

"Something that was very hard for me to get a handle on," says Margot, "especially right after he left, had to do with the fact that Jimmy is such a charmer. He really is a nice guy in many ways, and people gravitate to him. I've had a couple of friends say to me, 'Well, Jimmy has some flaws—hasn't everybody?—and he needs to do some growing up, but he told me the best joke the other day,' or 'he came over and spent the whole afternoon helping me reline the brakes to my car.' Then I start thinking, What was wrong with me that I lost this charming guy?"

• A new, better question: "Who can help me sort out his flaws *and* his virtues more clearly?"

If you're thinking, He *is* a nice guy, so it *must* have been my fault, find a friend or friends who can be counted on to give you a straight story and a true picture—someone who saw a lot of the two of you together, someone you spent weekends and partied with or who joined you at anniversaries, holidays, and barbecues over many years. Ask that friend or friends to help you with a little reality check.

Says one woman: "You want to take responsibility where you should take responsibility, and for me, talking to two friends was tremendously helpful. They gave me some pretty objective feedback. They didn't say, 'You were absolutely wonderful and he was an absolute jerk.' That wasn't true, and I wouldn't have believed it. But these people knew both of us well, and they were still telling me, 'You're OK.' That was a help and a comfort."

Margot found a male friend especially good for her reality check: "Men think and do things differently from women. For me it was a boon to talk to Alex, a guy who'd spent a lot of time with Jimmy and me during the four years we were together. He didn't take sides, but he was able to say, 'I know Jim well, and I've talked to him recently, and here's what I know about the breakup, and here's the perspective I have on it.' And he saw the weaknesses in Jimmy as well as the good stuff. This helped me sort things out in my own mind—I saw more clearly where to take the blame and where to put the blame squarely on Jim."

6) **"Why was I so trusting?"**

If you saw the signs of a straying man and asked questions and got fishy answers—*and* you believed them—you probably feel foolish right now. You wonder why you didn't rely on your good head and sound instincts and insist that you and he get to the bottom of things.

Says Maria: "People don't walk away from good marriages. I knew the marriage wasn't the best, for a long time. I did, several times, confront him. I asked him why he wasn't home more, I even asked if there was someone else in his life. And each time he'd look at me and say, 'No, of course not.' And I simply believed him.

"I was with this man for twenty years. He was the father of my kids. So I kept on trusting. Now when I look back, I think, God, was I a fool! Once you find out about the first lie, then you start to wonder if there was any truth at all. You think, Hmmm, that time five years ago when he said he had to spend the weekend in Chicago on business, maybe he was really shacking up with somebody at the Holiday Inn across town. And then you really feel like an idiot."

- A new, better question: "Is it a mistake to be trusting?"

Of course it's not, and being trusting doesn't mean being stupid.

A number of characteristics define a sane, healthy, active life. You cannot live in a state of amorphous fearfulness, for example; if you do, you won't drive your car, because someone might crash into it and kill you. Primary among the characteristics that define a sane, healthy, active relationship is trust. You cannot live in a state of distrust of the man you love; if you do, the foundation of the relationship is faulty. As one woman says: "If you can't trust him, who *can* you trust?"

If, like Maria, you catch yourself picking through the debris of the past and wondering which stories he told you were true and which weren't, tell yourself there is nothing to be gained from going back down that road, and resolve to stop.

7) **"Why didn't I leave him?"**

Or you *didn't* trust him all that much, you weren't all that eager to continue in the relationship, and you were quite certain that sooner or later he'd be gone. But you stuck around.

For many married women, of course, leaving is not a real option. Walking out takes grit, nerves of steel, some degree of economic security, and the conviction that your children will not suffer terribly from the breakup of the only home they know. Whether leaving was a possibility or not, you might still look back and feel dumb or weak for not having taken action yourself. And you'll feel angry and embarrassed as well because you're still the one who got left.

"I recognized certain signs," says one woman. "I knew it was going to happen, and the shoe could have been on the other foot—I could have been the dumper. But I chose to wait it out because I didn't want to be the bad guy."

Another was dumped after years in a deeply unsatisfactory marriage. When friends asked why she had stayed so long, Marina knew the reasons: her husband, she says, made a good income and provided a home; he wasn't much of a father because he was never there, but she was content to do all the parenting; and she had her own social life.

Still, her decision to wait it out doesn't make her feel great about herself: "I was actually relieved when he left, not so much for myself but for my children. Mickey, I felt, had become a terrible example—he was a drinker and a smoker and a psychologically abusive man. But really, I could shoot myself because I should have gotten out years ago. I am a strong person, but somehow I just did not know how to get away."

- A new, better question: "Could I, in fact, have left him?"

If you're berating yourself for having been too spineless to walk out on your unhappy marriage or your faithless lover, ask yourself whether that was a truly viable option. Many legitimate and admirable factors conspire to keep a woman in a relationship—finances and children, of course, and perhaps a deep sense of commitment to the promise that the relationship will continue.

Abby knows she would have remained in her marriage forever: "We took our vows in church, and that was sacred to me. I know I would never have left, no matter what happened."

8) "Why didn't I recognize what was right in front of me?"

Some women look back and see their own heads buried in the sand.

Says Barbara: "He was a lawyer, very busy, away a lot of the time, made a lot of money. I was a high school art teacher. There were so many signs that things were not good between us, but I never put the pieces together. I ignored it all."

Ann ran a cattle ranch with her husband, Ted, who for two years before he dumped her was having an affair with a young woman who worked for them. Ann never noticed until one day she found a woman's underpants in the truck Ted and their female helper often used to move livestock.

Perhaps you too are wondering why you didn't see what was right there and asking yourself, "How could I have been so blind?"

- A new, better question: "Why did I choose not to know?"

At some level you probably *were* aware of what was happening but developed a case of selective blindness.

Thinking it through, says Barbara: "I knew, but I didn't know. I have to admit, maybe I ignored everything in part because I was enjoying a very good life with him when he was around, and I liked it. We were flying to Paris on the Concorde, going to Wimbledon, going to Nassau for a weekend. I should have confronted him. Maybe subconsciously I thought, Do I want to just turn away from all of this?"

Says Ann: "If I acknowledged in my own mind what was going on and challenged him about it, then I'd be bringing us to a close and *I'd* have to leave. I didn't think it all out rationally, but looking back, that's the only thing that explains why I chose to ignore so much."

Maybe you saw and heard nothing because at an unconscious level you were holding on to the life you knew. It helps to recognize that now and to excuse yourself for what is, after all, an understandable instinct of self-preservation. Besides, almost certainly the signals that were coming at you were mixed, conflicting, and intermittent; they could be clear *only* in retrospect.

9) **"What made me get together with him in the first place?"**

Maybe you're looking at your ex now and wondering what you were thinking of when you first decided to share your life with him. Maybe you had a strong sense at the outset that the course of your relationship was never destined to run smoothly, and you made your decision with blinders in place or for reasons that had little to do with love.

Karen says: "My one and only husband, who moved out ten years ago, was actually out on the town with another woman the evening I was in the hospital having our one and only child, fourteen years ago.

"For me, the difficult aspect of his cheating and eventually leaving was not embarrassment and not seething hurt or anger but a sense of personal disappointment about the choice I made. I think I knew really from the start that he was not an especially good person. I chose someone whom I didn't particularly like or respect. But he was a physician, I was thirty-six, I wanted to get married, I wanted a child. I suspended all those reservations. I wasn't true to myself."

Says another woman: "Looking back I see that I didn't really *know* a whole lot about him. He didn't tell me a lot about himself. There were signs, even before we decided to live together, of the kind of person he was, which I might have picked up on had I been older or more experienced. For example, there was always a nasty streak about Adam, and he wasn't always honest with me or with his friends."

- A new, better question: "Was he, in fact, not the man for me?"

Sometimes it happens. Says one woman: "I did not expect him to walk out on me, I did not want it to happen, but after the split, I saw very clearly how different we were. I think he's now probably with a better person for him. It's, like, apples should be with apples and anchovies with anchovies. And I think that he and I were definitely an apple and an anchovy."

Don't spend any more time faulting yourself for picking the wrong guy. Even if you suspected you were making a bad choice, chances are you gave the relationship every opportunity to succeed. It didn't.

10) "Did I expect too much from my ex?"

"I don't know," says Zoe. "Sometimes I think I wanted it all—a great lover, great friend, great listener. And he should make decent money, be something of a jock, and also do some laundry and take out garbage. And you shouldn't expect to get it all."

It can be easy now to suspect that what you did wrong was to weigh him down and finally turn him off by measuring him against an impossible standard.

- A new, better question: "What was the bargain between us, and did I fulfill my side of that bargain?"

Give this some thought. If you had expectations of him, so did he of you. Most relationships proceed with certain implicit expectations or assumptions. Analyze the basic assumptions in yours. Perhaps they were that you'd each contribute equally to the finances, that he'd do house repairs and you'd keep in touch with the relatives, that he'd cook and you'd clean, that he would leave you alone a lot and you would leave him alone a lot, that you'd both try to stay fit and healthy and looking good.

Whatever they were, did you, by and large, keep up your end of the bargain? Did he, by and large, keep up his end? And if he came up short, did you, on the whole, let it ride?

You may find, as did Zoe, that your expectations were really few and basic after all. She says: "I honestly feel that I did everything that was expected of me. And as for him, he was a good friend and lover, at the beginning, a so-so listener at best, and a slob around the house. But what I *really* expected of him was that he be there for me, be honest, and work with me to build a life together. And he chose not to."

• • •

Sizing it all up, one woman reached her conclusion: "Of course, there are always two sides to a story. I was not his dream woman, which would probably be some combination of Julia Roberts, Sandra Day O'Connor, and his mother. Here's what I think:

opportunity came, and she was younger and cuter—
and it was too tempting."

Reach your own conclusions, and tell yourself
that in whatever way you contributed to the end of
your relationship, it was not *all your fault*. If you
believe it was all your fault, you are in danger of
clinging to the notion that you can make it better
and *patch things up*. And then, of course, you are
not moving on into your new life.

While you're still ruminating about what went
wrong—ideally once and for all—let's consider what
may have been in your dumper's mind and soul.

We've talked about *how* they dump. Now let's
examine *why*.

Dumpers: Why They Do It

- He was tempted by someone cuter and younger.

If he was hitting middle age, maybe your ex was
starting to feel discontented with his life. He'd
reached many of his goals (or few of them), and
they'd turned out not to give him the satisfaction
he'd anticipated. He was worrying about downsiz-
ing or heading for retirement. He looked at himself
in the mirror and thought he saw his father. And—
here's the big one—his sexual powers were flagging.
He was ripe when opportunity came along.

"A man, when he gets to be forty-five or so, his
dick isn't so hard anymore—he's scared," says a

woman whose boyfriend of nine years walked. "He feels his whole life is sinking along with his dick, and he's desperate to get out and grab some more life and some sexier sex. He can't get that with his old girl-friend, so he finds a new body."

- He's caught up in a grand romance.

Sexier sex goes along with romance, and he's titil-lated by the romance and excitement of a new woman. A typical predump scenario—he's married and he and she live in different places so that they must meet and talk on the sly—is conducive to romance and passion, which is only inflamed by the inability to be together. Passion is not inflamed by the routine of walking the dog or putting the newspapers in the recycling bin each night.

- You remind him of matters he'd rather forget.

We've heard this lietmotiv from many married dumpees—you're the woman he associates with dif-ficult days. Perhaps there were big money worries, you struggled together to solve them, and you thought everything would then be fine. In fact, you remind him of the struggle period, and he'd rather be with someone who doesn't. Coming through hardship together, contrary to expectations, can do terrible things to a marriage.

Says one woman: "He had a series of business setbacks over the years. At one point we lost almost all our assets and had to start over and rebuild, which we did. I think around that time he made a conscious decision to *really* start over again because he didn't want to look at me. He wanted to be with somebody with whom he had no history."

Says another: "Hal ran into someone he thought appreciated his worth a lot more than I did. We had gone through difficult times with one of our children, with doctors and child psychiatrists and testing and the works. Although our son is doing fine now, Hal never came to grips with the situation and still hasn't. And he met a woman who's young, sweet, eager, and brings no child pressures."

- He's not in his right mind.

Maybe because of the grand romance, he's in no shape to make rational or morally decent decisions about his life. A few dumpers, as we've noted, suffer through a great deal of Sturm und Drang over their betraying and unfaithful actions. In such a state, he's vulnerable and likely to go along with the agenda set by the new woman, which involves scrapping the old and moving in with the new.

One woman's ex visibly suffered guilt and indecision during the months when he was deciding what action to take. "I'm not trying to get him off the hook," she says, "but I really believe that Sam was unbalanced when he decided to break up with me. I know that if he were here now, he'd say it was the most traumatic thing he ever went through, a difficult, painful time for him and a big crisis in his life."

Says Annie: "When a man is under incredible

stress, he'll often make decisions he wouldn't make ten weeks later. Mark told me he could not live with himself any longer in this lie, and I know that emotionally he was totally out to lunch. He was a wreck—for as long as I was. I don't know how he functioned at all."

If your ex is one of these, you may find some consolation in the thought that he didn't know what he was doing and was powerless to alter the course of events. Don't, however, let this thought derail you.

- He changed.

If you're wondering what was wrong with you to love, believe in, and sleep with a man who turned out to be such a worm, let *yourself* off the hook by considering that very likely he once *was* lovable, believable, and worthy of your passion. You didn't make a big mistake; he changed.

"I have thought a lot about the twenty-some years I was with Michael, and I can say there were ten when he was a terrifically nice guy," says one dumpee. "The next five he was not so nice, and the last five he was a stinker. I think it's good to think of people in sort of different time components. The man I knew and loved madly was a different person from the man he is today."

Marianne echoes that thought: "I think Kent is happy with his new girlfriend. The thing is, he's happy in a way I don't want to be happy. He's changed what he wants from life. He says now he never wants kids, never wants a house, doesn't intend to put a hundred percent into his job. He says he just wants to have fun. I think he's being honest—but this is not the guy I knew."

- He's genetically and/or emotionally programmed to be unfaithful.

We toss in this possibility because a number of dumpees believe it. Says one philosophically: "Maybe a man can't stay with one woman from the time he's twenty-five to the time he's sixty-five. Maybe he can be with you for ten years and that's the life of the relationship. I fully expect that most men will move on after a seven-or-so-year period if they stay that long. And I'm now OK with that. My ex and I could have ended up friends if right at the beginning of all this he'd said, 'I really think you're not the woman for me, and I'm not the man for you. I'm going to leave.'"

Even if you might agree that men can't be faithful over the long haul, does that excuse the reality that your ex lied or cheated or played games with you? It doesn't.

- He dumps because he can.

When, for any of these reasons, a man decides to move on, there is not much that will stop him. The ease with which a man is able to dump one woman and find a new one has a lot to do with statistics and societal mores.

Some research says that 15 percent of committed married men don't play around; or 85 percent do. Others put the figures at 30 percent/70 percent. Whatever the exact truth, we can certainly make the general statement that a lot of married men seek female companions outside their marriages.

Some scientists trace the root of this infidelity back to our ancient hunter-gatherer pasts, when men had to procreate with many women to ensure the survival of the species. In our not so ancient past, unfaithful men—unlike unfaithful women—have not been much taken to task for their wandering ways. To the contrary, wandering ways have often been considered part of the package that forms the aggressive, ambitious, successful, dynamic male.

That male usually has his pick. Women who today are between the ages of thirty-five and fifty-five are at the mercy of numbers and the age-related pecking order: women typically marry older men, as men marry younger women. Given the roughly equal but vast numbers of males and females born during the boom birthrate years between 1945 and 1960, men have more to choose from the older they get, and women have fewer.

But here's something else to explain the dumping epidemic. In the old days, unfaithful husbands usually played but stayed with their wives—the Joseph Kennedy Sr. syndrome. One prominent New York financier was recognized by his pals as a master of the Long Island Railroad Shuffle: pleading a need to return to the city for urgent meetings, he'd kiss the wife and wave goodbye to the kids after lunch on Saturday, board the train at Easthampton, get off the train at Southampton, spend the rest of the weekend with his mistress, and then on Monday take the early train into Manhattan.

That's not the way they do it anymore. With virtually no public embarrassment or ostracism attached to walking out on your wife, today's married dumper divorces number one and moves on to number two (or three) with relative ease. Paying for multiple households may give him pause, but he's unburdened by worries over social reactions.

•   •   •

Now that you've tallied up your rights and wrongs, you're pretty sure, if not firmly convinced, that you weren't *all* wrong. You've considered what *else* might have motivated your ex to dump you, and you think he was on his way out for reasons of his own. Nevertheless, you may *still* be waiting, perhaps subconsciously, for it all to be over.

Can I Get Him Back?

One woman realized suddenly just what she was doing: "For weeks after my boyfriend left, I would lie in bed at night trying to read and I'd 'hear' a key in the front door. I would jump up, excited, rush into the living room—and, of course, there was no key. I would have a small plunge into gloom and then go back to reading. One day it occurred to me that my behavior was pitiful. At the time I couldn't stand the thought of seeing him. And here I was at night saying, 'Hooray, he's come back!'"

Says another: "Every time I heard a car door slam outside I'd think, 'Oh, you've come home, you silly goat.' But it was never him."

Don't worry about it too much. Hearing a phantom key is like feeling pain in a phantom limb. The limb is gone, but a few twinges linger on. You'll get over it if you give yourself a firm talking to. If you have been truly and thoroughly dumped, he is not coming back. You don't need to buy a book on surviving your lover's affair. You are not a case for "Can this marriage be saved?"

Says one dumpee: "My first advice for the newly dumped woman is, face the fact that it's over, this is a wake-up call, get on with your life. Women who sit around hoping that the guy will come back get stuck."

Accepting the wake-up call is harder when your ex is making sounds as if he's on the fence. The dumper who stews over his decision to move on may actually be troubled by the pain he's inflicting. He may be anxious about his ongoing affair—living a lie takes its toll—so he blurts out the fact that there is someone else. Or maybe, when it's finally time to fish or cut bait, he's full of self-doubts.

Your ex might be one of these if he tells you he never planned to break up the relationship, he's trying to end it with the other woman, he does want to stay together, he *thinks* he wants to stay together, and so on. He leaves your home but doesn't move in with her; he gets a three-month sublet somewhere or bunks at a friend's apartment. He says he's trying to straighten things out.

Larkin's ex fit this picture: "This is a guy who's always had a lot of trouble making decisions, a guy who flips a coin to decide what he's going to order in a restaurant. And here he was faced with a huge one. He went back and forth for nine months—did he want Larkin or did he want Suzanne? What if he made the wrong choice? What if he dumped me and then Suzanne didn't work out? He did not act like a grownup."

A married dumper, after announcing somberly to his wife, "I am in love with another woman," ended up remaining in their home for the next ten months. During that—for her and she thinks for him too—miserable stretch of time, he often declared that he still loved her, it was just that he was *in love* with someone else. She calls this the worst time of her life, a time when she felt like a puppet on a string, juggling routines, keeping up the semblance of a marriage.

In retrospect, she says: "I should have handled it very differently. I should have kicked him out on day one. But I loved him, I couldn't believe the marriage was really ending, I believed what he was saying, and I let him do this to me. Finally I got smart and said he had to make a decision. Now he's married to her."

Should you wait it out or call it quits while a

man on the fence wrestles with his passions or does whatever he needs to do to arrive at his next move? If you still love the guy, can get beyond his betrayal, or have other reasons to try again, you're probably wise to give him some time and space—telling yourself at the same time that chances are he will leave at the final curtain.

Counseling might help. Or it might not.

Even if a dumper claims to be undecided about what he wants, he may agree to counseling for any of several reasons, conscious or unconscious, none of which is aimed at you two getting back together. Many dumpees say the man will submit to therapy in order to:

1. Let you down more easily and give you time to adjust to the idea that the relationship is over
2. Look good in his own or others' eyes
3. Speed up the process of his leaving (he may find it more comfortable to be in a therapist's office for a "confession" of feelings and actions that will convince you he's emotionally invested elsewhere)
4. Get professional "proof" that the relationship is damaged beyond repair

Says one woman: "We went together for a number of sessions with a couples therapist, and I understood we were there to try to put the marriage back together. It sounded as if that was his wish too—at the first meeting he announced, 'I had an affair, I am still seeing the other woman casually, but I would like to figure out what happened with us and rebuild,' etc. Looking back, it's apparent to me that we were there so he could talk himself out of the marriage and tell himself he 'tried.'"

Go for professional help if it seems like a good idea, but remember, your ex-man is way ahead of you: he already knows there's another life out there for him, and whatever mental wrestling he did over trying to make it work, he did long ago. At some point—and if you're clearheaded and not deceiving yourself, you'll know when that point is—decide that nothing's getting better and enough is enough.

That's what happened with Larkin: "The way I deal with pain is to make a deadline in my mind, a time past which I will not continue in a losing situation. I went to Mexico on a vacation, and I told him, 'By the time I come back, either you live here and make the relationship work and get rid of Suzanne, or you get all your stuff out and make a complete break.'

"I went to Mexico, came home, he wanted us back together. I said, 'Can you guarantee you'll end it with Suzanne?' He said, 'I'll try.' I said, 'Not good enough.' And that was finally the end of it. It was almost as if he needed me to make the decision for him."

•   •   •

Perhaps you still suspect:

- "No one else on earth has been such a fool for love as I."

This is not true. In fact, a great many intelligent, competent, attractive women have been even bigger fools. If you still need proof, you can skip ahead right now and read Chapter 7. You'll feel better.

If You Have Children

Nine Rules to Promote Peace and Security

The fact that you're a mother has an upside and a downside at this point, especially if your children are still quite young.

The pluses: They are undeniably *there* and must be fed, dressed, bathed, put to bed, and sent to school on time. They impose a structure on your day and compel you to take actions and do good restorative things, like make dinner on a fairly regular basis, that you might not necessarily do on your own. They love you, you love them, and they're so nice to have close by when you need someone to hug.

On the minus side: The evening you are in the mood to do nothing except have a good wallow could be the evening of the PTA meeting. Child-rearing must continue to absorb most of your energy and attention at a time when you're coping with your own emotional upheaval—and later, when you're hoping to find new friends and figure out how to socialize again. The dumper father, if he wants to remain involved with his child, will be a bigger part of your life than you might wish. You must talk to him often about weekend visits, school schedules, and other details, and you must see him when he comes to pick up or drop off your child, when you'd be happier right now if he lived in Outer Mongolia.

But whatever the plus and minus aspects of your life as a mother who is also a recent dumpee, your children inevitably will be struggling to adjust in these early weeks and months. Their mom is often sad or angry or distracted. Their dad is living somewhere else. When they spend time with him, perhaps a new woman is there, too. Their grandparents are upset. Their old routines are disrupted. Everybody's acting a little crazy.

Your children might prefer, passionately, that you and their father were still together. They might be blaming themselves for the fact that you and he *aren't* together. While they're still stunningly and appropriately egocentric, young children find it natural to hold themselves accountable for the disintegration of the only home they knew.

Says one dumpee: "Right after my husband left, finances were the most obvious and pressing problem, and the kids couldn't help but be aware of that. And my daughter thought for the longest time that what happened to our family was her fault because we'd spent money on her riding lessons and horses. My son thought it was his fault because he attended a private school. That's been the biggest worry in all this, that the kids blame themselves."

Teenagers, say many women, often have an

especially tough time making sense of and coming to terms with what's happened. They may work hard at remaining carefully neutral, or they may take sides and give the disfavored parent a lot of grief.

The mother of a girl who was fifteen at the time of the split remembers that her daughter became suddenly hostile toward her: "She was always a daddy's girl. She was wounded, and she turned on me. She'd say, 'If you were such a wonderful person, why did Dad leave? Why wasn't he happy with you? Why does he have somebody else?' She didn't talk to *him* but took it all out on me."

Much has been written about the children of divorce: how to tell them the news, how to establish custody, visitation, child support, and other issues affecting the dissolution of the family home. Certainly if your children seem to be going through a prolonged rough patch—unnaturally quiet and "supergood" or angry and acting out, having trouble in school or problems sleeping or eating, unusually fearful and worried—you must inform yourself about ways to help them and perhaps invest in short-term professional counseling, for them or you or both.

In this chapter we focus on the dumpee-dumper connection. Divorce is always wrenching, but the fact that you were *dumped* complicates the task of helping your children through this passage in some very real ways.

Dumpees we have talked to, many of whom learned through their own mistakes, say the following nine rules are most important for providing children with as much peace and security as possible.

• • •

1) **Don't say bad things to your children about your ex.**

This is critical and difficult.

Says one mother: "You don't want to steer them against their father and poison that relationship. But here you are, extraordinarily hurt and angry and perhaps without many people to talk to, and here are these children, who are upset and sympathetic to you. It's hard to stop yourself from saying things you will regret. But you must take the high road, even if you have to grind your teeth to do it."

When you think you absolutely *cannot* stop yourself from saying something rotten to your children about their father, stop yourself. Run to the phone and call your support person immediately, and tell *her* what a rat he is. If you attack Dad, *you* will be the one who is harmed. Every opportunity to trash him that you pass up will rebound threefold in your favor.

Erica's children were four and eight when their father walked, and over that bad time she developed a mind-set that helped: "Pretend you're in a Noel Coward play. Be civilized. Never have your war with him in front of your kids. Unless he's a total stinker, your kids love you *and* him, and you don't want that to change. You made those children with Dad, and to do an about-face and bad-mouth him to them is absolutely off limits. You and he screwed up the marriage. Now your responsibility is to *not* screw up the kids."

If your children have to form conclusions about their father, they'll form them on their own. As time goes along, they might want to talk more. Feel your way along—but don't ever put him down, if for no other reason than that they'll come to resent you for it.

2) Be honest, as best you can and to the extent of your child's capacity to understand.

Stopping yourself from telling your children what a jerk their father is doesn't mean you should pretend all is well. Obviously it's not. Parents often think they must display nothing but upbeat, cheery emotions in front of a child because kids get upset to see a parent upset. They *do* get upset, of course, and they prefer you upbeat and cheery, but they can end up feeling even worse if Mom assures them that what they think is going on isn't really going on.

Says one woman: "You must communicate some sense of reality. Although it's a tough line to walk, you can't just say everything's fine and then carry on and be the wounded mother. Kids are not stupid."

Remember, though: your children don't need to know what you *really* think about their father. "I have a friend who's going through this right now," says one dumpee, "and I've heard her say to her kids, 'Your dad's a cheater and a liar' and so on. She says she's not trying to carry on a vendetta, she's just being honest and telling her kids what she feels. I think she's doing real damage. I've seen this happen—her children become quiet and look away when she goes on the attack."

Your children have enough to deal with right now. Give them as straight a story as you can.

The main points to get across: Dad is not going to be living here anymore. I hope you'll see him often. If you have questions or want to talk, come and tell me. Sometimes I'm going to be in a really lousy mood or I'm going to be feeling sad or angry, but remember, none of that is because of you.

3) **Explain, a little, about the new woman in Dad's life.**

When your children are very young and your ex will be seeing them on a regular basis, and it's up to you both to make the arrangements, children should be prepared simply for what is to come. Say something like: "Dad found another woman he likes very much. He is living with his friend [or "When you go to see Dad tomorrow, his friend will be with him"]. I'm sure she will be nice and she'll think you're very nice. I hope you'll have a good time. And in case you're worried about it, she will not be your mother, because I will always be your mother."

Just let your child know this person is on the scene, and try to answer any questions as simply as possible. There may be no questions.

Many dumpees say their ex-husbands revealed nothing to the kids about the new woman and suggested instead that they were leaving because "Mom and Dad aren't getting along too well," or they needed to have some time on their own to sort things out. Those children were then upset or startled by the sudden appearance by their father's side of a strange woman, or perhaps someone they'd known.

Says the mother of a twelve-year-old girl and a ten-year-old son: "My daughter knew things were going wrong between her father and me, but when he left, all he told the children was that he wanted to have his own apartment for a while and he would be getting it all ready for them to visit.

"Then the first day they went to stay with him, *bam!* there was Sophie, their dad's assistant, whom they had often seen over the past year— and she's also living in this apartment! My daughter later told me she realized her father must have been having an affair for a long time before he left. She was devastated."

It shouldn't be your responsibility to explain his affairs to the children. It may turn out to be, however, and it's better for your kids if you supply them with a few facts ahead of time than to leave them in the dark.

4) Try not to ask your children questions about their father.

Most women say that the more you quiz the kids about Dad, the more they clam up. Although they'll talk to you when and about what they want, they loathe being expected to report in. If there are reasons you need or want to know about your ex-man's current life, you must ask him yourself.

Says one woman: "The kids would come back after being with their father, and I'd ask them about him—how was he, did he say how his business was going? And I realized this was awkward and painful for them."

She made the effort to reestablish contact with her former husband, and now they meet occasionally for lunch or coffee: "I can see him comfortably now and get an update myself. My being civil made him prepared to talk and share information with me, and I can leave the kids out of it. They really don't want to get involved."

5) Don't quiz your child about the new woman.

How your son or daughter and the new woman hit it off and what they think about each other will develop over time and out of sight. For everybody's sake, hope they get along agreeably and that she's a caring person who pays attention to what's best for your child.

Right now, find ways to promote that desired state of affairs, and be on the alert for stumbling blocks. For example, in the early days after being dumped, especially if you don't know much about the new woman, the temptation to ask your child what she's like may loom large. Acting on it is a bad idea. You're picking at the scab once again, and remember, you want a good clean scar from your wound. In the bargain, you're probably making your child uncomfortable.

If your children are old enough, it might be wise—at a calm moment—to have a short talk with them, fess up to the fact that you've been subjecting them to a grilling, apologize, and resolve out loud to stop doing it.

6) **Help your child maintain contact with Dad.**

Most dumpees we've questioned feel strongly that they want their children to have a continuing relationship with their father. If all is going smoothly, your children see him regularly and happily. Visitation drop-offs and pick-ups are arranged smoothly, and it is all relatively free of tension. If this is your situation, count your blessings.

Often all does not go smoothly. Some dumpers—usually the workaholics who were never terribly caught up in their children's daily lives—find it difficult or tension-making to maintain contact with their kids, so they seldom call or visit. If your ex is one of those and your children are emotionally the poorer for it, perhaps you can help them to nurture more involvement.

Says one woman: "They saw very little of him. *I* was bitter, but I didn't want bitter kids, and I didn't want them alienated from their father. During the early years, I put a lot of effort into keeping them in touch. I'd say, 'You haven't heard from Dad in a while. Why don't you give him a call?' Or 'Have you told your father about the essay award you won?' I knew their father didn't feel connected and involved and that it was painful for him, but my main thought was that it was healthier for the kids to encourage contact. And I believe it has paid off. They're older now, and they view him affectionately and perceptively."

If your ex really doesn't want much contact with his children, there's not a lot you can do about it. Don't try to convince them that even though he's nowhere to be seen he's thinking about them. They will find no reason to believe you and won't admire you for your efforts.

Says one woman: "I used to tell my kids constantly, 'Your dad really loves you so much.' And finally they started telling me, 'He loves us at his convenience and on his schedule, so stop patronizing us.' I learned that lesson—it's up to him to show them that he cares."

These disappearing dads sometimes come out of the woodwork for special events. One man left his wife and two children who were just heading into high school, had no contact with them for several years, then appeared out of the blue at his daughter's graduation. The daughter thought it was great, he posed for pictures looking like a proud poppa—and his ex-wife was speechless and furious.

There's not much you can do about the special-events Dad either, except try to be happy if your child is happy.

7) Don't allow yourself and your ex to slip into bad guy/good guy parenting roles.

If your children, as is typical, live with you and visit Dad on weekends and holidays, possibly you and your dumper have fallen into good guy (him) and bad guy (you) parenting roles. Time with Dad is all fun and games; when your children are there, they get to stay up late and eat pizza three nights in a row. Time with you is all "clean your room and do your homework."

First, be a little more of a fun guy yourself. Allow a one-hour transition break when your youngster arrives back with you after time with Dad: relax the rules and regulations, watch a cartoon, have some laid-back time together.

Then, push for changes. Very young and school-age children require fairly consistent eating and sleeping schedules or they go haywire, so you have the right to request and expect compliance from your ex concerning daily routines. Try to talk to him peaceably, not right after your child comes home wired from lack of sleep or excess of sugar and you're furious. Make one of those careful phone calls to his office on Monday morning, and tell his assistant: "I need to talk to George briefly about our daughter, and we can do that this afternoon or tomorrow afternoon." Have ready the list of changes you believe need to be made in your child's away-from-home routine.

8) Insist on equal treatment for your children in Dad's new home.

If he's setting up housekeeping with Barbie *and* her kids, do not be surprised if those children in various small ways become the "real" ones and his child becomes the outsider. Some dumpees say their youngsters get short shrift in their father's new home, even from a loving and involved Dad.

Betsy's husband left her to move in with (and later marry and still later divorce) a woman with two young sons. Betsy says: "When Ben, our son, went to spend weekends with his father, he slept on the living room couch while the other boys had their own rooms. And Ben could never have his father all to himself. They were always going out to the museum or the ballpark or whatever as a unit. I know his father was trying to promote closeness among them all, but Ben sometimes felt he'd lost his dad."

You can't talk to the new woman about her kids versus your kids, but you can and should talk to your ex. Give him the benefit of the doubt, as Betsy did, and assume he's largely unaware of what's going on and doesn't mean to move his own child to second-fiddle status. She wrote a letter marked *Personal* to her ex's office outlining her objections, being careful to list some comments Ben himself had made that indicated he didn't feel entirely welcome in Dad's new home. Dad, who loved his son, listened and made some adjustments.

If matters don't improve, don't read the riot act to your ex. This is a situation that can be helped by some short-term counseling. Insist he join you for a session with a child psychologist or other objective third party, and try to work out some specific solutions.

9) Be happy if your child likes the new woman.

When your youngster comes home after a weekend away and talks about how pretty and nice Dad's new friend Barbie is, your nose gets out of joint fast. For the good of your child, you must develop a neutral attitude, or at least pretend to have one.

When your little boy starts enthusing about Barbie, train yourself to sit down with him and say, "Tell me what you all did this weekend." Listen with a smile on your face. Still smiling, say, "Well, I'm glad you had a good time, honey. Now let's read a book." This will be hard, but you'll feel like a saint.

Even better, be glad that he thinks she's nice. If this woman is going to remain a permanent part of your ex-husband's life, she'll have a lot to do with your child, and you perforce will have a lot to do with her. You'll be grateful to her for your child's sake.

Says one dumpee: "I've actually come full circle. Over the years, I appreciated the way she was with my children. The kids were happy over at their house, and it was she, really, who made that happen. I'd phone my former husband and say, 'What's on for this weekend?' And we'd have a typically dumb conversation—'I don't know, I've got to work,' blah, blah. So I ended up calling her more often, and we'd work it out. She'd say, 'OK, I'll get Jenny to soccer on Saturday afternoon and to the party Sunday, no problem'—and so on. I guess she realized when she took him on that she took my kids on, too. And they are very fond of her."

Their getting along is in everybody's best interests, so be glad of it.

Post-Dumped Parenthood: When Life Gets Easier

When you're still in the earliest stages of creating your new life, this can be hard to picture, but at some point down the road you may be tickled pink to watch your children take off for a weekend or a two-week school vacation break with their father—leaving you to your own devices.

"My kids were my security blanket; I didn't want to let them go," says a mother of two sons. "And when my ex came and took them every other weekend, it was terrifying to me—a whole weekend, what was I going to do? What I found out is that those are the times you truly rediscover yourself. So eventually I was saying, 'Phew, they're gone for two-and-a-half whole days!'"

Later still, it got even better: "I've got to say, it was *really* nice when my kids were old enough to drive and could go off on their own to visit their father. That's when I started to lead a really independent life."

Four years after the big dump, Jane, a mother of three, sees where they've been and how far they've come: "I remember in the beginning the children yelling and acting out a lot, me crying at three in the morning, wondering what in the hell was going to happen to us. Then I got stronger because I had to, and the children did, too. We had to relocate and pretty much start over in many ways. And now they're fine.

"The children *do* survive. If you are strong, to the best of your ability, it rubs off on them, and it does work. That's what I'd like to tell a woman who's just starting to go through this—children are flexible and tough, and they survive."

6

Midway Slump

What to Do When Everyone but You Has Lost Interest in This Saga

You're over the emergency period. But while on some days you don't think about him once, on others you're suddenly back again in the fetal position. After a good stretch of time, out of the blue comes an absolutely hideous day, perhaps triggered by an innocuous event—you learn that friends from your couple days went on a ski trip with your ex and his girlfriend, or your ex and Barbie just returned from taking the children to Disney World and the kids are loving them like crazy.

Nobody wants to hear about your hideous day, because nobody has your story on the front burner anymore. People tend not to be judgmental about others' relationships, which is certainly all to the good since life must go on, but it doesn't make you feel better. In fact, it really plunges you into despair or thoroughly pisses you off.

Catherine says: "The anger you feel is intensi-fied by the fact that so many people seem to have an accepting 'Oh well, that's life' attitude. In my par-ents' day, the man who left his wife was a sinner! Someone to be shunned! Now, the man takes off on Tuesday, shows up with the girlfriend on Thursday and says, 'This is Kimberly'—and everybody says, 'Hi, Kimberly.'"

You're still looking for a little retribution, and none is heading his way.

Your primary supporter is sending clear signals that enough is enough already. Friends are tired of hearing your story. People are implying or outright saying that it's not a big deal—when you know it damn well is and it should be.

"My experience has been that people will give you about six months for a grieving period," says a woman who's about eight months into getting over it, "and after that you're on your own as a social being."

Says another dumpee: "It's fine for a short buzz, and then you're ancient news. This is good on the one hand because you don't want your private life to be a hot topic. On the other hand, sometimes you *do* want to talk about what's happening, and you feel constrained and fear you'll come across as a bitter bore."

Some older unmarried dumpees feel they get particularly little attention; friends, they say, don't understand why they can't "snap out of it." Says one: "I lost a fantastic loving eleven-year relationship when Brian found someone new. And the people I knew seemed not to be able to acknowledge that I was hurting. Dumped wives get sympathy. Dumped girlfriends or love partners don't."

Where once they were sympathetic listeners, now your friends are getting a little testy. Where once they let you talk and gave you a hug, now they're offering advice—you should get out more, or look for another apartment, or tell off your ex-mother-in-law.

Maybe even your own flesh and blood is losing patience, as was the case with Ginny: "I was in pretty bad shape for a long time. It was so bad that my sister would often check in first thing in the morning, just to say, 'Hi, kiddo, how are you doing?' One day she called and asked how I was doing, and I said, 'Not too well, actually.' And she just snapped over the phone—'Smarten up! Get over yourself! What's the matter with you?' That hurt!"

But you still *need* the willing ear. You want your friend or sister to know how you feel. It's become clear to you that recovery is not an upward curve; your pain isn't going to go away quickly, and some of it isn't going to go away at all. But your friend doesn't understand why you keep retreading old ground, why you aren't "getting on with it." You *are* getting on with it but not the way she thinks you should.

Friends may also be expecting you to be what you were before—what, in fact, you won't be again. Life and loss have changed you; you are evolving into someone new. Says one woman: "My friends would probably describe me now as being 'better,' in the sense that I go out a little more—not as much as I once did although certainly more than in the first months after I was dumped. But I am not the same person. A friend said to me recently, 'I want the old Charlotte back,' and I said, 'She's not there anymore.'"

So if you're not in the direst of straits any longer, you're still in fairly murky ones. Everyone else, especially your ex, has adjusted nicely to the fact that your relationship is history.

This is the point at which you can slip easily and unwittingly into a posture that does you no good, turning into a viper or a turtle—or perhaps each in turn. The viper snaps at anyone with a fairly good word to say about the man who did her wrong or anyone she thinks isn't acting properly supportive. Even if she originally held her tongue and rose above it all, she's finding that harder to do now since people are acting as if *nothing happened*. The turtle pulls her head, arms, and feet deep within her shell, unwilling to deal. Either one is *not* the way to go.

Although you've hit a bump on your road, you don't want to be a viper *or* a turtle. This is a time to reshape your social life, a time for new action, a second wind, perhaps even a bold, outrageous stroke or two.

Let us now explore how to get over the bump in the road.

The Midway Slump:
16 Ways to Beat It Back

1) **Listen to yourself carefully.**

   If you seem to be turning people off a lot lately and you're often peeved at the lack of responsiveness from friends, ask yourself:

   Have you made your support person or crew your therapist?

   Are you playing the same old record over and over?

   Are you and your woes all you're ever in the mood to talk about?

   Do you think your friend is being an insensitive jerk when she changes the subject to describe the terrific date she just had or the plans she and her boyfriend are making for a vacation in Cancun?

   If the answer to any of these is yes, work hard at putting an end to your behavior. Ration the time you spend rambling on about your saga, especially as time passes. Go back and see the therapist for a couple of sessions.

2) **Consider what aspects, if any, of your old social scene are still pleasurable for you. Let go of the rest.**

   Many women are buoyed up by the continuing affection and attention of a solid group of old pals. Some—especially older married dumpees without major money worries—even find they now have more time and emotional freedom to nurture and enjoy their friendships. If you're in that well-equipped boat, be glad of it and cherish the people who can love you without trying to fix you.

Possibly, however, like many dumpees, you now find yourself socially at sea because, when you're dumped, couples stuff usually ends. Two or three of your former joint friends may have come down firmly in your court or his. Most try not to take sides, and those friends will invite your ex and his new woman to the parties, the beach weekends, and other "big ticket" events. The more successful he is, the more likely he is to be "forgiven," picked up, and kept on certain invitation lists.

Marion found that several really good girlfriends stuck with her, but she was deeply disappointed by a number of other people: "These were people from our jobs and a couple of volunteer groups that we worked for—people we'd seen together for a long time, and they all just disappeared. My ex was a big fund-raiser, and I think a lot of these people sort of went with the flow or whatever, and they vanished. I was complaining to my therapist about this, and it was the only time she got cranky with me. She said, in effect, 'Get real—that was business, this is life.'"

You're almost certain to hear about events that once would have included you and now include him and the woman of his choice. Says one woman: "My former husband and I were very much part of a social scene. Now he is and I'm not. Some people we've known for years have a summer fiesta party, as they call it, every June. This has always been a great affair, very posh and elegant and fun. This year Jonathan and his girlfriend were there, and I was home with the kids." She doesn't like it, she says, but accepts this displacement as a fact of her new life.

Those same friends may have *you* over for dinner with just the two of them, so you're a little threesome. Or you're invited on family night, with the barbecue, the grandparents, and the kids. Although this is nicer than not being invited at all, perhaps it leaves you feeling resentful or down in the dumps. Certainly it can't help but remind you that, in this Noah's Ark world, you've been pushed off the boat.

Be true to your feelings. If you're genuinely fond of the couple who want you for dinner, and you can be relaxed and up for some nice food, wine, and talk, go and have a pleasant time. If you feel unbearably tense about it all, don't go simply for the sake of being polite.

One dumpee thinks it's impossible to keep up a social life with friends who are also socializing with the ex-man: "I've tried this, and it really doesn't work. There's not the same feeling of trust or whatever. There are people I know who see Sean from time to time, and I can't go to their homes and enjoy myself and feel open with them, knowing he might be there next Saturday and someone might repeat something I've said. I think in these situations there's almost always a separating of the couple's friends."

Laura has discovered this about herself and the invitations of old friends: "I don't like being a third wheel at a dinner party that often. I find it uncomfortable, and I don't like reciprocating, so I'm just as happy to be relegated to the B-list, so to speak—to go to the casual family gatherings or the cookouts with the kids."

Don't take all this personally, she adds: "Be careful not to blame people. When you're on your own and you're not being included in stuff much anymore, it isn't because those friends don't like you. You just don't fit in as you used to."

If you haven't heard from someone whose company you enjoyed in the old days and who you realize, perhaps because of business associations, is going to remain in your ex-man's camp, you might want to say, "It was nice knowing you." One dumpee says she found a satisfying sense of closure by doing so: "I wrote letters to three couples who had been in our lives, people we often saw at functions connected with John's business. I just said, essentially, 'I'm pleased that I had the opportunity to get to know you, and I enjoyed the good times we had.' It felt good. Two of these women wrote me very sweet notes, and I had lunch with one. I doubt I'll keep up with any of them, but this was better for me than simply, bang! I'll never see or talk to those people again."

Don't become bitter. Cara says that while she was married she gave thought to her single friends and always tried to include them in her entertaining plans: "Two of those women are now married to men they met in my house. And since I've been dumped, neither of them has invited me to so much as a dog fight."

Let it go. The people who aren't calling or the invitations that aren't coming are part of your former life. Maybe they'll come back at some future date, but don't spend a lot of thought and energy on soliciting social support that's not there. New people will be in your life soon.

3) **Learn how to handle irritating invitations.**

- A friend calls and says, "Gary's in Los Angeles for the week on business, so I'm free as a bird. Want to go out and get something to eat?"

  If you'd enjoy the evening, go. If you're hurt by the fact that these days she only thinks of you while her boyfriend or husband is out of town, let her know without getting viperish.

  Meet for dinner, and at some point you will see an opportunity to say, "You know, we all had some good times together, and I miss doing things with you and Gary." She might feel a bit uncomfortable by this reference to the fact that you've been dropped from the couples' list, but if she's a genuine friend she won't hold it against you, and you'll feel better for having gotten it off your chest. That's something you'll be doing more of in your new life.

• An old friend says, "Give me a call sometime, we'll get together."

Call once or twice, and if she's unavailable, vague about her schedule, or unwilling to make a plan, forget about it. Assume she was just being polite.

• A friend calls and says, "A bunch of us are going up to Boston for homecoming. Why don't you come and bring a date?"

Friends who have been married or paired off for a while, who haven't had much contact with other than couple friends, don't grasp that you don't *know* a man you'd bring to a festive occasion right now and haven't a clue about how to find one. Says one dumpee: "A lot of couples, I've found, are in a very different space. They look at you and think you've got all this freedom, you're on your own, you can invite whomever you want. They don't understand the reality of your situation."

You might reply: "Thanks, but there's no one I want to bring right now." Then you'll probably spend some time talking yourself past this new little blow to your self-esteem because you're wondering, "What's wrong with me? How come I'm not a woman who can say, 'Right, I'll just call up Joe or Harry or Fred'?"

Very few recent dumpees can. There's nothing *wrong* with you.

4) Decide you *will* find the time for a new social life.

Says one woman: "Going to someone's place in the evening requires planning. You're working full time, and suddenly you're also maintaining the house and the yard and the car, so going out somewhere for dinner is way down on the list. I probably *should* be doing more of it, but it doesn't seem to happen."

Another woman says that her life is occupied with her job, her three-and-a-half-year-old child, and a few good friends. But she has few single women friends and neither the time nor the stamina to nurture more: "It seems I have my career clothes and my Mom clothes—now I need my single-babe clothes and my single-babe activities. That's a piece of my life that's missing. My son is my priority, and I'm fine with that, but when he's away on a weekend I think it would be nice to have some fun. Except I'm too bushed anyway."

If you hear yourself making similar protests, be careful. Lack of time can be a problem, but don't let it become a defeating one. Don't use it as an excuse to be a turtle. Carve out time for socializing—then forge ahead.

5) Take the bull by the horns; begin the reordering of your social life.

OK, so you've been feeling lately like the odd person out. Clearly you have left your social life too completely in others' hands. Regain control. Focus now on building a life with others that doesn't have to be partner-centered.

If you've been sitting around waiting for people to call you, take action. Maybe a friend you'd like to see doesn't know that you'd enjoy being asked over for pizza or going out to a movie. Maybe the last time you talked to her you couldn't imagine leaving your apartment, and she's waiting for you to give the signal that you're back on track. Make some calls.

Pull out that list you made a few months ago of people you want to see more of. Think of someone you would like to know. Cold calls are hard to make, but if you've heard about a friend of a friend you'd like to meet or you remember the interesting woman who sat across the table at a think-tank luncheon two years ago, look her up. What have you got to lose? And over the long term, you may gain much.

Four years after being dumped, Ellen finds herself with a better social life than ever: "I have a much larger circle of friends now than I did in my years with Jack. Our friends then were almost always people he liked, and a lot of them were guys he'd gone to school with and their wives or girlfriends. Most of those people are totally out of my life now, and I can't say that I miss them at all."

Another woman realized that in her pre-dumped days she always had places to go and people to see but never felt much need to: "My unit was my family, my husband and my kids. After he left, it occurred to me that I didn't have many close friends. That scared me— being out there by myself. I'm slowly making friends. I know now I have the capacity, I just never put in the energy. Now I'm putting it in, so I'm getting it back."

6) **Don't spend *all* your time with other women.**

Perhaps you've found that the group forming around you in recent months is largely made up of women—divorcées, recent dumpees, single women—who'd like to compose a social life with you. They don't want to be alone on Saturday night, and they're calling you to do things together.

This is fine, to a degree. You *will* be spending more time with other women than you did when you were part of a couple, and you'll enjoy their support and companionship. But don't get locked into every-Friday-night-drinks-with-the-girls; don't become excessively caught up in taking historic homes tours with nine other women. Do all that if you really want to *and* the all-female activities are not becoming your only social outlet. Your new life will not be couple-centered, but you also don't want to cut yourself off from half the population.

7) **Search out men as friends.**

You need men in your life—not men as in "the new man," or as in the date or the walker, but as in a coworker, your brother-in-law's single brother, your friend's accountant. Nice men who will help keep you from souring on males just because you happened to run into a lemon, men who will be good and perhaps helpful to talk to, and who will validate that you are a woman men enjoy.

It's a cliché (with, of course, truth to it) that the dumped woman becomes the target of unwanted sexual overtures from married or attached men, whose women are therefore threatened by her. Sometimes it works that way; often it doesn't.

One dumpee made a point of keeping in touch with a couple she'd known for several years. She says: "Jim and Barbara are a great pair, solid as a rock, and they've both always been affectionate and wonderful to me. Jim often puts his arms around me and gives me a hug. Nobody thinks there's anything 'going on.' When you've had a man in your life and now you don't, it's just nice to be touched and comforted this way by a male human being. I don't feel he's my friend's boyfriend—he's *my* friend."

Another woman valued contact with her brother-in-law during a time when she was deep in a midway slump and working at shoring up her battered self-esteem: "You can have a feeling, 'Am I totally unattractive and incomprehensible to every male out there? Do I do something that makes men run the other way?' I remember having a long talk with my sister's husband and saying, 'You understand what I'm talking about?' and him saying, 'Yes, of course I do.' And I thought, Well, maybe it's not me versus men. I can talk to other men—it's just my ex, the man I was trying desperately to talk to, who couldn't hear me."

8) **Invite people to your place.**

It may take you a good long while to work up to this one. One woman says she used to entertain a great deal during her married days and enjoyed having people to her home: "Now I don't entertain at all. In fact, I've had friends over once in the past year. It still seems too much without the live-in host and extra pair of hands. I hope this will change in time, but we'll see!"

Says another, three years after being dumped: "I almost never have parties or dinners anymore, except some old friends in for drinks now and then. Very occasionally I'll invite some people over to return social favors, but I don't have a light heart in the process."

If you feel similarly leaden-hearted about the notion of entertaining, maybe you need to stop trying to repeat old practices and find new ways of doing things. Paula says that two years after her husband left, she decided to have some office friends and a couple of old pals over for dinner. It was not a smashing success: "First, it was expensive. Second, I made an impressive-sounding and complicated main dish that I'd never cooked before. I felt hassled all evening. After everybody left, I stayed up late, cleaning up and weeping."

A year later, she tried again: "I had some new friends by this time, singles and divorced people. I asked a couple of people to bring wine, somebody else to bring a dessert. I made chili the night before, and we had that and salad and bread. Everybody, including me, had fun. I don't sweat entertaining now. The point is to maintain contact, not to be Martha Stewart. Although, now that I think about it, I heard she got dumped, too!"

Rid yourself of other couples' notions, such as that people come in pairs. Mix, don't match. One woman says: "Don't worry about balanced groups. I've had parties where I invited a whole bunch of people, and for whatever reason we ended up with two men and maybe ten women. And it was a great party, and of course those two men had a wonderful time."

Says another: "About two years after I was on my own, I got the courage to throw a Super Bowl party for a few people. It wasn't nearly as difficult as I thought, and after the evening was over I wrote in my journal that I had just crossed another milestone in the recovery process."

9) **Get out there.**

Calling people is good. Hosting a get-together in your place is good. But more and more often during your midway slump, you must also get out there and make the scene, whatever your particular scene may be. Don't hide in the house, even if a lot of the time that's just what you feel like doing. Withdrawal is destructive and will turn you into a turtle.

Says Gail: "It's the women who stay home who get out of the circle very quickly. The longer you sit home and watch television or whatever, the more uncomfortable it becomes to get out and do things."

Sometimes, she says, you have to force yourself: "I've made myself go on a trip or out to some function and then thought, Oh God, what am I doing here? But you know, I've been glad I did it, every single time. Fake it till you make it. People don't have to know you're anxious or nervous. Play the role. Pretend to be relaxed until eventually you *become* relaxed."

Don't be too hard on yourself. This is a difficult time. Says one woman: "I learned not to expect a whole lot of myself. I make myself go out, sometimes when I'm not really in the mood for it, because later I'm almost always glad I did. But if I go out and decide I want to leave, I just leave. I don't beat myself up over it."

On the other hand, *never* staying home can be a problem, too. A few women look back on their early postdumped days and wonder if they were in the grip of a mad and mindless compulsion to remain in perpetual motion.

The woman whose husband made a public announcement of his new love—and who therefore found, she says, that "the entire city was appalled by him and supportive of me"—was inundated with lunch, dinner, and party invitations: "I wouldn't turn anything down unless I couldn't be in three places at the same time. It was the most exhausting summer of my life. I was also in no mood to eat, lost thirty pounds, and couldn't stand to look at myself because I looked as if I had come out of a concentration camp. I had a mirrored wall in my bedroom, and I'd walk in the closet to get changed and then go charging out to some event." She pulled herself up short just when she was in danger of burning out.

Another woman remembers: "For some time after my boyfriend left, I'd get in a panic thinking, There's a weekend coming up with nothing to do. What can I do! Then I'd sign up for a seminar or something the day before, rush out of town, just to get myself over a weekend—and end up sitting on a rock crying."

If you staggered through your walking wounded stage barely able to drag your head off the pillow and now abruptly find you've catapulted into frenzied activity, if you're looking at your calendar determined to fill up each evening and weekend, slow down and give some thought to what you're doing. Are you getting enough sleep and living in a healthful way? Are you out on the town or out *of* town so you won't be back home feeling abandoned?

Dashing around to dinners, movies, clubs, and other busy places may indicate that you're frantic and desperate. Better to be frantic that way than to run off to Acapulco and have affairs with beachboys, but it is a sign that you're terrified of being alone.

Stay home some night and get back to writing in your journal. Recording your thoughts and feelings in that notebook intended for no eyes but your own can be restorative and soothing in a midway slump.

Put on some good music, lie down, meditate, and drift.

Think of someone who could use your ministrations. Says Jean: "When I'm having an anxious night, I make a big pot of black bean soup and a lemon cake and bring them to an elderly neighbor who lives in my building."

10) **Bite the bullet: go solo.**

You're invited to a swell affair—a fancy wedding or black-tie evening—and it will be your first such outing without your ex by your side. Without any man by your side.

Go. While you may feel uncomfortable, you'll definitely feel worse if you pass it up from lack of nerve. At this point on your road to recovery, you're not likely to get weepy at an unfortunate moment, and others are not likely to stop their conversation and stare at you, because, remember, people are no longer fascinated by the fact that you're a dumped woman.

Get in a suitable frame of mind. One woman who's always done a fair amount of lively socializing says that in her predump days she often went solo because her husband was away on business—and she thought nothing of it: "It was perfectly comfortable for me to be there on my own because I could say, 'Stanley's in London.' Now I'm there on my own because Stanley's in bed with someone else, and that has made me self-conscious."

She imagined wives were considering her a threat since she was now presumably available to their husbands. Finally, she got over it: "I thought, This is ridiculous. First of all, what's the difference? Alone is alone. Second, I'm not after anybody's husband, and probably nobody's thinking that I am. Just in case, I always make a point of chatting up the women more than the men."

The prospect of going solo gets stickier if you think or know that your ex and his new woman will be there, too. If you can work up a fair degree of mental fortitude, and if the affair will be large enough that you can avoid sitting next to them, go and try to have a good time. Other people may find the situation a bit awkward, but that's not your problem.

Says Arden: "This was a very big holiday party, and my ex was there with his girlfriend. The party was going on throughout several rooms. I stayed in one, they stayed in another. And people came to both locations—to pay their respects, sort of like a funeral."

At the time, she says, her emotions were still a bit too raw to see the humor in the situation. Later she thought it was a hoot.

After the evening is over, say many women, comes the difficult time. Says one dumpee: "I miss the pillow talk. I miss coming home from a party and not being able to do a number on the people who were there, who said what to whom, who was looking good, and who made a fool of himself."

Be prepared for feeling down in the dumps, even after a good night out. Put on a funny movie, drink some warm milk, and try to get to sleep as soon as possible.

11) **Know your down times; be somewhere else.**

A woman who gloomily contemplated the approach of her first postdumped Christmas decided to get out of town. She rounded up three unattached friends; they rented a double room at historic Mohonk House in upstate New York for the holiday weekend and spent a great three days in a crowd of friendly strangers, singing carols, drinking eggnog, and hiking the trails.

Getting out of town isn't possible for everyone, of course, but if time and finances allow, plan ahead to be somewhere really nice other than your own living room and bedroom on your anniversary, birthday, or any other emotion- or memory-laden day.

If time and finances block getting out of town, try to be *anywhere* other than home on those days. Help the needy. Says one woman, "Look only five degrees to the right or the left, and you will see that there are far worse things than getting dumped." Sign up for a bird-watching walk—getting the endorphins pumping will do you good, and maybe you'll meet a potential fitness buddy with whom to start a little fast-walking morning regimen.

12) Seek out his other women.

The more people you can meet who don't know your ex, the better, but here's the flip side of that: look up the one or two you haven't met who know him perhaps only too well.

This tactic is not for everyone and may sound slightly grotesque, but connecting with an ex-man's *other* dumped woman or women might be helpful at this stage. There's a real plus to finding out that someone else was taken to the emotional cleaners by your former husband or boyfriend. You feel a little less like a jerk, because you have company. You enjoy a unique relationship with her, and the two (or possibly three or four) of you might benefit from sharing a few laughs or commiserating over life with and without George.

Says Eve: "Bill and I had been divorced for several years when one day, out of the blue, I got a call from Kate—the woman he left me for and later married. She was in tears. Bill had just dumped her! We've met for lunch several times, and we've actually become rather close. I was able to help her through the miserable period in the beginning, and now when we get together we end up laughing about how ridiculous it all seems.

"I used to see Kate as the temptress who wrecked my home, ruined my marriage, and stole my husband. I despised her. Now I see the whole picture differently. Getting to know her has helped me finally bring that whole period of my life to a close."

Barbara, another dumpee, tells this story: Bob, her boyfriend of six years, announced that he was moving out of their apartment and moving in with Linda. Sometime later, Barbara learned that another woman had been equally upset by Bob's betrayal—Alice, his girlfriend of three years. Says Barbara: "So I was apparently not even *in* the debate. His dilemma was, do I leave Alice for Linda? It turned out that I had had no substance in my relationship at all and for a long time."

Barbara looked up Alice; they talked, they met, they compared notes. They had a good time.

If there has been another ex-woman or two in your ex-man's life, you'll hear about her. As we've noted, people let you know what they've known for years and now feel free to reveal. If you don't find looking up his ex a weird and appalling notion, try it. If you do, forget it.

13) Consider a crutch.

Hillary, the head of her own small public relations firm, says this about her midway slump:

"After about a year, although I was generally in good shape, I often had difficulty concentrating. I'd be in a meeting, and suddenly my mind was somewhere else. I'd be obsessing about some ancient details of the whole relationship mess."

Another woman says she was doing just fine until her ex-husband took their two children and his girlfriend for a month's vacation at the family's summer house: "This was the first time Matt took Pat to the island—to stay there, to sleep in our bed. This was different than if they were in a hotel or an apartment in another city. I could not get my mind around it, couldn't stop focusing on it."

These setbacks can hit you hard and slow you down. You've exhausted your support system, you're suddenly thrown by some new development or persistent thought, and there's nobody on duty to help you get over it.

If you've followed the *Dumped!* advice and have been avoiding medications, this might be the time you can benefit from some. Says Hillary: "I had ferociously rejected the idea of taking anything to ease me through the bad early time after my boyfriend left. I was reluctant to rely on something 'false.'" Now she talked to her doctor, who suggested a mild antidepressant that she found of great help during this bad stretch.

Don't think you're a superwoman. You may truly need a crutch, and that's all right. Talk over options with your doctor. You may end up not filling the prescription, but it's nice to know it's there.

14) Confront the ghost of your ex-man.

Although you're in a midway slump and working to get over the bump in the road, you *are* stronger than you were at the beginning of that road. And especially if your recent efforts to reorder your social life have been paying off, now may be the time to move your ex-man a little further into the past.

Call up a friend, and invite him or her to join you for dinner at "your" restaurant or for a walk in "your" park, the places you and your ex frequented that you assiduously avoided in your early dumped days and that you haven't been back to since. Go, look around, and decide it's just a place to eat or walk after all. Superimpose a new memory of a pleasant afternoon or evening over the old ones. Consciously deromanticize.

Pick a quiet weekend afternoon to dig out that carton of memorabilia of your relationship. Take your time, go through it, and allow yourself, if you need it, one small, ideally final wallow as you remember the love you shared. Then decide what you will keep and what you will toss. If you want to hold on to it all, that's fine; pack it up, put the box back in the closet, and forget about it.

If you decide there's no reason to hold on to this stuff any longer, that's even better. Says one woman: "I had to have a burn. I got down my box full of his letters, pictures, some poetry books he had given me, cards that came with flowers, *Playbills* from shows we'd seen, all this stuff. Then I had my burn. I built a fire—which was itself a big deal because Tom always made the fire. Then I sat in front of the fireplace with a bottle of wine and drank my wine and tossed everything into the fire except for two photos I decided to keep. It was a purging experience."

15) Get a new look.

You've been thinking of having the eyes lifted or getting a little collagen here or there. You avoided making such major body-altering moves during your walking wounded phase. Consider making them now.

Buy a fabulous, sensuously cut suit.

Get a great new haircut.

Whatever you do to improve your looks at this time, you'll do as part of a clear-sighted move toward your new, better life—not in a knee-jerk reaction to the pain and fury you suffered when your man left you for another woman.

16) Read your diary.

That notebook with the tear-splattered pages that you started three or six months or a year ago, wrote in every day, and haven't reread—get it out now, turn back to page one, start reading, and see just how far you really have come.

Look at your "Fifty Things I Want to Do" list. Decide that by this time next year you will have checked off at least one or two of those items.

Decide that your midway slump is over.

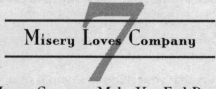

Misery Loves Company

Horror Stories to Make You Feel Better

If you're moving smartly and confidently on with your life, skip this chapter. If you're still feeling alone, enraged, or embarrassed and you're not above taking some small satisfaction from others' disasters, you may be buoyed up by these horror stories.

Many of the dumpees we've talked to have candidly and ruefully told us personal tales of betrayal that will curl your toes. For some of these women, getting back on two feet—financially, emotionally, and socially—has required extraordinary measures of time, effort, and resolve.

Reading their stories, in their own words, should persuade you that you have not been the biggest patsy of the century and that if *they* can survive, you can, too.

Angela, age 44

After many years of money struggles, things seemed to be going fairly well for Peter and me. He had a small electronics business that we had built up together over the years, and now a conglomerate was ready to buy it. Peter was exhausted, busy at all hours working out the sale. For the last three years, our two kids seemed to be seeing him only in passing. His life was one major meeting after another.

One Sunday afternoon I finally got his attention for an hour, and during our talk he agreed that our family life was suffering. He suggested that we start making things better by going, just the two of us, for a couple of relaxing weeks to Hawaii. The paperwork for the sale was finished; the deal was set to close in six weeks. It was with a light heart that I called a travel agent and made plans for what sounded like a dream vacation.

Five days before we were scheduled to leave and two days before my parents were arriving to look after the children, Peter said the deal had hit a few last-minute snags that might delay his getting away. He had a suggestion, he said—Janet, my closest friend, could come with me for the first week, and he'd be there for the second. Janet was divorced and on a tight budget, so Peter offered to use some of his many airline points for her ticket.

While this plan certainly didn't sound like the second honeymoon I had been counting on to help Peter and me get connected again, it did have its attractions. Janet lived a four-hour drive away, and we didn't get to see each other often.

Janet arrived the night before we were to leave, and she, my parents, Peter, and I all had a pleasant dinner together. The next morning she and I flew to Hawaii, feeling up and almost as young and silly as we had in our early college days. We got to Maui, settled ourselves in the condo, and poured our first mai-tais. The next couple of days were terrific. On the third evening, Janet told me I was in for a treat—she'd made reservations at the best restaurant on the island. It was Peter's idea, she said, and he'd given her the money for this special dinner.

So we drove to a place that resembled a plantation house and settled in for a memorable meal. Everything was beautifully served and tasted wonderful. Janet said that Peter wanted her to order after-dinner drinks, and then she had something for me. I expected some sort of present until Janet handed me an envelope with Peter's writing on the front.

I opened it, read it, and thought, I will die, right here in this restaurant. Peter said he was leaving me. He had met someone else and realized that one has to seize true happiness when it presents itself. He was sorry, but he knew I was a strong person. I would surely realize that our marriage had not been good for a long time. He knew we could arrange the financial settlement in a reasonable and calm manner. He told me to stay until the end of the week and then come back all rested to handle the situation at home.

Janet was looking at my face as I was reading and kept saying, "Angela, what is it?" I don't remember how we got out of that place, and poor Janet was a wreck, seeing me so unhinged. When I showed her the letter, she was horrified. She had been totally in the dark, just told to arrange a special meal on the third day and hand me this sealed envelope. Somehow we got back to the condo. I cried all night and finally slept a little near dawn. The next morning I called Peter's office and was told that he had gone on a fishing trip with the new owners and couldn't be reached.

Although it sounds odd to me now, Janet and I stayed in Maui until the week was over. Then we came back and I faced the music. My parents, also in the dark, were wonderful. Peter basically dropped out of our lives for a while. It felt as if he was away on a business trip. Most of his clothes were still there, his desk was still in the den—it was just that he had set up housekeeping with a young lawyer who had worked with him on the sale of the company.

Why couldn't he tell me himself? How could I have been married for sixteen years to such a coward? I still don't know the answers to those questions.

We reached a financial settlement, got divorced three years ago, and he is now married to the lawyer. Although some of our friends were appalled when they learned how I got the news, he and the new lady are seen around town, and no one seems to be making any judgments about what happened. While my children are not happy with the situation, I've taken them to counselors, and they're managing as best they can. Peter now sees them according to a formal schedule.

I found a job through a friend who owns a dress shop, and I volunteer at a women's shelter. Between busy days at the store and seeing others who are in worse shape than I am, I think I'm coming to grips with what happened. I can't even *think* of another man at this point. That is something that will come, if ever, after I am over my war wounds.

Alana, age 28

After graduating from a community college and taking some intensive computer training, I applied for and was excited to accept a job working for a man who was opening a new restaurant in our city. This was David's second restaurant; his first, opened three years earlier, was a smashing success, and David was flying high. He was dynamic, aggressive, confident, full of plans and phenomenal energy. He was ten years older than I, and compared to him, the other men I knew seemed shallow and uninspired.

From the start I put in almost as many hours a day as he did, setting up computer systems for purchasing, personnel, and all aspects of this business that I found increasingly fascinating. After almost a year of working together, it seemed that David and I were in the restaurant more than either of us was anyplace else.

I was thrilled when he said he wanted me to go with him to a trade show out of town. That trip was heaven. For three days, we worked the show, ate in every restaurant we could find, and talked about all those details of our lives that enable you to get to know someone. I guess it isn't surprising that we became lovers.

The next few years flew by. I had found, I thought, not only the man for me but a promising and exciting career. David and I almost always closed the place together each night, then spent some after-hours time hanging out and talking shop with others in the business. Although he kept a tiny company apartment near one of his restaurants, four or five nights a week we were together in my place.

We were in our fourth year as a couple when I started having odd physical problems—occasional blurred vision and then some small difficulty with balance. I chalked this up to exhaustion for a long time and promised myself to take a vacation sooner or later. Eventually I got myself to a doctor, then spent a fair amount of time going through various tests.

At first David was understanding and solicitous—then increasingly impatient with me, even cool. I think now that he probably suspected long before I did that my ailment was fairly serious. One afternoon I arrived at the restaurant to find that he had hired a new assistant to make the workload, he said, "easier for you to handle."

Things happened fairly quickly after that. I was diagnosed with multiple sclerosis. When I tearfully told

David the news that very evening, he insisted I take a medical leave. It turned out he had already talked to his insurance agent and started the paperwork. He was distant and impassive as he was telling me all this. I found it difficult to absorb what was happening.

I left the restaurant just like a docile lamb. I felt as if I were sitting on a beach, just watching wave after wave roll over me.

Time passed. My doctor gave me antidepressants, and the MS is now, mercifully, in remission. David has elected to drop me from his life, and I haven't seen or heard from him since I returned to the restaurant to sign some termination papers and collect my things. I lost my heart for that whole line of work and now work as a programmer for an accounting firm.

I have dated casually, starting about two years post-David. Things are going fairly well, and I feel quite content as I live my uncomplicated life. I almost think of the person I was then, so swept up in this man's world, as another person. I think I like who I am now a lot better.

Ellen, age 53

Sam and I had a nice life. My father had helped Sam financially when he started his real estate business, and Dad also bought us a lovely house, right on a golf course, after our first son was born. As the years went by, Sam's business grew, and he became involved in larger and larger projects.

Everything was going along swimmingly until a property downturn in our area meant that the houses Sam and his partners built weren't selling. My father had the majority of his money tied up in real estate, so now he had problems, too. Then suddenly things seemed to go from bad to worse. One day my father had a stroke and was dead before nightfall. My mother and I were grief-stricken and then surprised to discover that she was left with less money than she thought she would have. Sam and I tried to support her emotionally, although business worries kept him busy and unavailable a lot of the time.

We went on this way for three years, and then one day Sam suggested that we sell our house to ease some of the financial pressure. My mother was moving into a retirement community; the boys were away at college and had plans to move elsewhere after graduation. It was time to start thinking about ourselves, my husband said, to get a small perfect house that would fit our lifestyle as we got older by being easy to manage and allowing us to do all the traveling we had always talked about. I liked the idea—a fresh start for Sam and me and a new site for our future life.

Meanwhile our own house had gone up in value, and it sold for just over a million dollars on the second day it was on the market. I started looking for our perfect small house and came up with some lovely possibilities. Sam, however, found something wrong with each one. He suggested we rent a place until we found the one we wanted, and he'd put the money in the market. My father had put our house in my name, so when I received the check from the sale I gave it to Sam. We rented a place, and I continued my search for our dream home.

Exactly three weeks later, Sam came home and told me he was leaving me. Plus, he was sorry to say that he had lost the million in the market. He found this so upsetting, he said, that he was leaving town.

It's impossible to describe how betrayed I felt. I learned later from Sam's secretary that he had been having an affair with a woman who had been a temp in his office three years before. It also turned out that he had been planning this whole scheme for over two years. Unbeknownst to me, he had sold his business to his partners, telling them we were going to get out of the rat race and travel.

When I was able to lift a hand and call the bank, I discovered there was less than four hundred dollars in our joint account. I couldn't even keep up the rent on the place where we had been living! I ended up for a while in an apartment over the garage of a good friend.

At this point my mother has given me thousands of dollars for lawyers, but we don't seem to have progressed very far. Sam and his friend, Bonnie, are living in another country, and he maintains that he lost the money in the market. I've decided that I can't afford to pursue it much further.

With the support of friends I have acquired a real estate license, and I've actually made some sales. I'm beginning all over again, and this time I'm counting on no one but myself. While I worry about the example Sam has given our sons, they realize it's something they will have to come to terms with on their own.

I've made new friends. Two months ago I sold a house for a nice widower, and we've met a few times since. We've talked a little about my experience, even laughed about how ghastly it was. I think this is progress, and I'm feeling fairly optimistic these days.

I will not *permit* myself to let Sam and his actions ruin the rest of my life.

Catherine, age 35

Richard and I both had great jobs, a nice condo, and we traveled to someplace odd and exotic at least once a year—a good life. Although we talked about getting married "someday," we were in no rush. Neither of us particularly wanted children, for one thing.

Rich got a promotion, which pleased us even though it meant he had to be away for about a week each month. When I wasn't busy at work, I'd go out with my friends more, doing things that wouldn't interest him, like seeing movies with subtitles. He started going to hotel gyms while he was out of town and working out. This resulted in his losing weight and developing an interest in eating the "right" foods. I loved the idea that he was taking good care of himself—I even took a course in how to prepare low-fat appetizing meals.

One evening Rich arrived home with a lot of fancy gear and said that on our next exotic vacation we were going on a wilderness camping trip. This didn't appeal to me at all, but Rich was determined, and he talked me into it. Besides, I thought we weren't quite as close as we used to be, and certainly a week in the deep boonies would give us an opportunity to catch up.

A small float plane flew us into a remote location—the plane would return for us a week later. So there we were in the woods. The first two days went fairly well, although I was bothered by the fact that Rich kept wandering off to survey the next hill or whatever.

On the second evening, I made a special meal with goodies I had brought with me as a surprise, including two bottles of his favorite wine. I envisioned a romantic dinner and a love scene like the one in *Out of Africa*. The stars were out, there was a new moon, and I started to think that maybe this trip was just what we needed.

While Rich said all the dinner fuss was silly, he seemed to enjoy it, and we drank both bottles of wine. Then he looked over at me and said, "There's something I have to talk to you about, and I think now is a good time." He proceeded to tell me that he was in love with his executive assistant and that she was three months pregnant with his child.

Looking back, I truly do not know why my heart didn't stop. I couldn't breathe, couldn't think. How could he do this to me? How could he do it *here*? How would we get through the next five days before that plane came back to pick us up?

I've blocked out much of that time before the plane came for us. I remember either sobbing or being numb. He kept saying he hadn't wanted it to happen, it just did—and telling me how much being a father would mean to him.

That was three years ago. Rich now has a son, and he and his former assistant live about fifteen miles from me. I bought a new, smaller condo, changed jobs, and lost myself in my work. I spent many months asking myself and a series of counselors how I could have been so wrong about a person. The answer to that seems to be that there is no answer.

About a year ago I had a brief affair with someone I met through business, a man who made me think I was attractive after a long time of feeling like something on the reject pile. He was married, which made me feel guilty—I'd think, What did his wife ever do to me? While I'm glad it happened, I'm also glad I decided to end it. I don't have the stomach for cheating.

Recently I signed up for a gardening class and met a nice man there. We're going on a regional garden tour this weekend, and who knows—maybe I'll want to plant tulips with him next fall. I accept that I will never entirely get over the fact that Rich betrayed our commitment. I regret that I didn't really consider having a child, but I can't do anything about that now, and I would question my motives for trying to be a single mother. I'm open to new ideas and new people, however, so I'll see what develops. Any man in my life has to have only two things—a sense of humor and a promise *never* to go camping.

Heather, age 36

I met Alan when I was in junior college and he was in graduate school. He was and is adorable looking, and I fell for him on sight. We dated for two years and had a terrific sex life during that time. We were married right after he graduated with a business degree. I got a job in a health clinic, and he started working for a software company. I couldn't have been happier.

Three years after our wedding, we had a baby girl, and two years after that, a son. I kept on working each time, after a short maternity leave, with my mother looking after the kids. Eventually the baby-sitting was more than she could handle, so Alan and I decided it would be best if I stayed home with the children and tried to get some home-computer work.

Although I loved nurturing my children, it seemed I was always exhausted when Alan got home. He kept telling me to be patient, soon we'd have enough money to give me time off. Month followed month, and it seemed all we talked about was news of the kids. We still had an active sex life, and I put any lessening of frequency down to our full schedules.

One day a good friend told me she had seen Alan having a friendly looking lunch in a suburban restaurant with a blond woman. I was annoyed with her and told her that of course he had to wine and dine clients as part of his job. All this time I continued doing what I thought was my part of our marriage, making a small income and looking after the children.

For our anniversary in June, we always went out for a special dinner, and I really looked forward to our ninth year celebration. Alan arrived late, and the evening seemed to get off to a somewhat frantic start. He asked for an out-of-the-way table, a request that I thought was sweet and romantic. He seemed distracted during the meal, as I told funny stories about what the kids were doing and asked about his work.

After dessert, he ordered brandies, which was unusual for us. Feeling the effects of the booze, I started to really relax. I remember taking my shoe off and rubbing his foot—and he jumped, which struck me as odd. Then he looked away and said he wanted to talk to me about something.

The rest of that night is still in slow motion for me. I seemed to be outside myself, looking at the two of us. In a nutshell: Alan said he was in love with a woman he'd met three years earlier, when I was pregnant with our son, that they now had a one-year-old child together, and he couldn't stand living a double life, so he was going to live with her.

I started to cry, jumped up from the table, ran out to the parking lot, and started to walk down this country road. I thought my life was over. What would happen to me, to the kids? What would I say, what would I do? Alan drove up beside me and said I must let him drive me home. After my initial burst of energy, I felt close to collapse. We got back to the house, and he said he didn't want to upset me further, so he wouldn't come in.

I thought this was a terrible dream that I would wake from. It wasn't. I told my parents the next morning, and I realize now that all three of us were ashamed. We knew this would be a gossip item—my father is a well-liked minister in our community—and we were at a loss about what to say. If it hadn't been for Alan's new baby, I think my father might have killed him.

My dreams were over. We sold the house, and I received enough child support to get me through the first week of each month. I moved in with my parents, and my mother took care of the kids. I don't know what I would have done without my mother and father.

I now work full time and am going to night school to get my college degree. I'm thirty-six years old, and I sometimes feel I have the weight of the world on my shoulders. Alan and his new wife take the kids for one weekend a month, and I guess everyone is coping the best they can. Certainly a lot of people had to get unhappy so that Alan could get happy. I wonder if he thinks it was worth it.

All in all, though, I'm getting on with my life and starting to feel better about myself. While it's not an easy road, I have two great kids, great parents, and the strength to not let this defeat me. Two years after it happened, I had a dumb affair with a fellow I went to high school with. I guess I needed to prove to myself that someone still found me attractive. I hope there is another man out there for my children and me. If there is, he will get a woman who is ready for commitment and wise enough to know what that truly means. If a man isn't willing to earn—and keep—my trust, I don't want him.

●　●　●

Sharing experiences can be an important step on the road to healing. You may find it consoling to learn that some dumpees got the shaft in nastier ways than you—they say misery loves company. At the very least, know that there are many women in your figurative boat.

Your New Man (or Lack Thereof)

Land Mines and Lessons Learned

Are you ready for a new man in your life? Some dumpees are so occupied with the demands of job, home, or children (or all three) that pursuing a love life is low on the list of what's desirable or even possible.

Some women just aren't interested. Many dumpees we've talked to have discovered to their surprise and delight that they feel content—even gloriously free—as a solo act, at least for a while, and have more than enough going on to keep them involved and engaged.

Says one: "Life without a man is pleasant in many ways. In fact, more pleasant than life *with* a man. So in terms of the future, it's going to be one hell of a guy for me or no guy at all."

Says another: "Here is something interesting I've found true for myself and a couple of friends who also were dumped. Once you get past the early stage of feeling you absolutely must attract a man again, you start thinking it's better not to be involved in a big-time relationship. There are men in my life I enjoy seeing. The goal of marriage, though, isn't there for me. You're actually kind of relieved because independence feels so good. And you become truly comfortable with yourself. That's what men don't do. They jump from one bed to the next, and they don't find themselves. They *never* get it."

Whatever your feelings on this score, sooner or later, to one degree or another, you will probably be in the dating arena again. If you are working on a new life that you hope will include a new man, you'll want to keep on your toes and know what to expect, from yourself and from them, especially in the early stages of meeting, talking to, and becoming involved.

Are You Looking for a Man? If So, Why?

The question may seem to beg the obvious, but you might find it useful to spend an hour one evening thinking it over. If you've been feeling a little frantic about latching on to someone new, clarify your thoughts and calm yourself down by pinpointing the sources of those feelings.

> I want a man—
> To replace the one who left me.

Not a great answer. If you're compelled to fill up the space your ex once occupied because that empty space makes you feel incomplete, you're liable to make big mistakes, such as settling for some bozo just because he's there. One thing this whole ghastly experience should have taught you is that a meaningful life is possible without a man.

Because I'm lonely.

This is more of the same. Even if your days are full, you *are* alone now in a way you weren't before, and you may often suffer pangs of loneliness. It would be great if all that could go away rapidly, but it won't.

To boost my ego.

Again not a great answer. Although your ego needs some boosting, looking eagerly for someone new to love you, to make you feel better about yourself, is a prescription for disaster because of that vulnerability to bozos and other unsuitable types.

To do the guy things.

One married dumpee says that after her husband left, she felt in a terribly fragile state: "He took care of so much. I had never even been to the wine store myself."

Maybe you're thinking of the things *he* did that you assume you can't do or that you've never done before. If he was the one who bought the wine, took the car in for servicing, put in the screens, got the barbecue going, argued about a bill—don't worry about it.

Of course, it's *nicer* to be able to turn some of

the gritty stuff of life over to someone else, but that doesn't mean you can't learn to handle it on your own. You'll discover that much of what men do and make a big deal about, like the barbecue and the screens, isn't really such a big deal at all.

To have an escort.

This is a perfectly legitimate need. Especially if your business or social life includes lots of evening affairs, it's very helpful to have a man. You don't have to be in love, married, or sleeping with someone, however, to come up with a congenial fellow who has a good dark suit, knows which fork to use, and can talk intelligently. Later we'll think about who this individual might be.

To have sex with.

Satisfying your sexual needs is, of course, one of the best uses for a man. If you've been accustomed to sex, craving it is another misery you've been facing. Laura says that she was always sexually attracted to her boyfriend, and he, as far as she knew, was always highly attracted to her: "Our sex life was excellent. We made love a lot. After he left I was really scared. I'm still scared. I don't know when or if I'll ever have regular sex again."

You must be careful now to guard against doing dumb things, such as tumbling into bed with the first warm body that comes along. For now, you might do better to address your sexual needs in safer ways, as some dumpees we will mention have learned to do.

To have fun with.

A good idea. You need to have some fun, and why not have it with a man? Again, though, a man you can spend good times with doesn't have to be a man you will love and eventually marry.

To be my soulmate.

You may find him. You may not. You believed you had found him once before, and look where that ended. Try to start thinking in terms of finding not a soulmate but a kindred soul.

To marry.

If you were dumped by a husband, you're used to being married. You may marry again, or you may not. Age, both yours and his, is a factor.

In general a woman's chances of achieving a long-term marital relationship decrease with age: if you're twenty-six, your chances are excellent; thirty-six, good; forty-six, so-so; fifty-six, it's a low-odds lottery.

As we noted earlier, men have a larger pool of available women to choose from than women have of men. (One happy trend is older women/younger men, although it's probably one that's not going to last.)

Fifty-year-old men, for example, tend not to become involved with fifty-year-old women. The personal ads tell the story: "Fit, trim, successful 50-year-old outdoorsy man looking for fit, trim, successful, outdoorsy woman, 30–45." Says one still relatively young dumpee who's interested in finding a new husband: "I figured fifty would be hard, but let me tell you, forty-two is not a piece of cake either. The good men are married, the divorced ones are poor and scared, and the rest want to do your hair."

If you're an older woman who has for years been part of a large, active couples social scene that now includes some recent widowers, you may find a likely candidate or two. Those men don't like being unmarried and may turn to a woman who's been a comfortable friend (unless he's thinking in terms of hooking up with a youthful caretaker to see him through his old age). If you're interested in a man who has recently lost his wife, time your moves carefully—remember that it's always the second woman in the door with the casserole who gets him. (He's still feeling too loyal to the departed wife to go after the first one.)

You might be thinking that all this is unfair and that if you had taken the measure of your ex ten years earlier and gotten out when you were more marketable, you would have had a better chance of connecting with some adorable person. It *is* unfair, but you can't focus on what might have been; that attitude will exude negative vibes.

When you've clarified your thoughts and sorted out your reasons, it's easier to be clear-eyed and cool-headed about the men you *do* meet. One woman went for a while to a "newly singles" group, which she found helpful and where she met two men who (separately) invited her to dinner: "One was a lawyer, and one was a doctor. They were both in their early thirties, like me, and I was pleased and flattered to be asked out. I had several dates with each, and they were OK, but once I got to know these men a bit, I thought, God, are you boring!"

Another woman says that almost immediately after her boyfriend walked, she was asked out by several men she and her ex had known in college: "I accepted a few dates, had some fun, and it did a lot for my ego. Soon I realized that I hadn't cared for these guys when we were in school together and I *still* didn't particularly care for them. I didn't go out with them then, and I didn't want to go out with them now."

As you start out on your postdumped dating scene, here is the most important lesson to remember: There may not be another man in the role of lover/partner/husband in your world for a long time or perhaps ever again. It's better to say it out loud, acknowledge it fully, and build a new life from that perspective. You'll be happier. And you'll certainly increase your chances of finding a new man if you're not a desperate soul running around frantically searching for one.

Men: First Forays

In the early stages of dating, you may be amazed at the sexual currents in the air. Your antennae, which have been folded in on themselves, are out and waving again and picking up signals. These are actions you have been oblivious to lately, or if not oblivious to, merely amused or perhaps titillated by.

Sexual currents—a little flirting here, a little come-on there—can be fun and great for the ego when you're in a committed relationship and have no wish to act on them. But now, when you haven't had a "date" in a long time, you may be receiving signals that are scary or puzzling. You can easily make one of two mistakes:

• You see overtures that aren't really there.

It's understandable. You have been so insulted as a woman that you tend to seek reassurance, which sometimes leads you to imagine incorrectly that a man's attentions signal a definite interest in romance. You're in danger of making a fool of yourself.

• You fail to see overtures that *are* there.

This too is understandable. Your confidence in yourself as a woman who appeals to men, as a sexual partner, took such a hit that when you do reemerge, you are often not sure what is happening: I think this man is coming on to me—but no, that can't be right.

Clearly it's going to be important to read all this correctly because some real overtures—the ones, for example, that are coming from your girlfriend's husband—you will want to avoid. Other real overtures—the ones coming from an appealing and available man—you may want to acknowledge in a way that encourages the possibility of something nice happening.

One dumpee stopped in the supermarket on her way home from work to pick up dinner and noticed an attractive man who was also assembling a solo meal. He looked at her appreciatively: "I thought he was trying to catch my eye and maybe say hello, and then I thought I was completely crazy. I got to the checkout with my little veal chop and green beans, and suddenly he was right behind me. The cashier said, 'Are you two together?' and he said, 'Unfortunately, no.' And what did I do? I burst into an inane nervous giggle, paid up, and dashed out."

This kind of behavior will make you feel like an idiot or like the clueless fifteen-year-old you were a hundred years ago. You'll get better as time goes on. For now, accept that at first you may have trouble deciphering overtures accurately, which is what you must do if you are to act on them as you wish or as you should.

It takes time to be ready for a new man in your life. Even when you *think* you're ready, you may not be.

Says one woman: "I got to the point where I just really wanted to have a date because I thought I would never be involved with another man again, never sleep with anybody again, nobody would ever ask me out again. A friend introduced me to a fellow; we went to dinner. He was the nicest guy, but the evening was a total disaster. I couldn't cope with the whole thing."

She pulled back, got her mind off dating, spent more time in casual socializing with friends. A few months later she tried another date, and it went a lot better. Her advice for other newly emerged dumpees: "Talk to your primary support person or another close friend who will be candid with you. Although you think you're presenting a positive, healed persona, you may not be. Somebody who knows you well can probably sense with accuracy if you're ready for a new guy or still too much a basket case to handle it."

Meeting Men

We're not going to talk about sports bars, singles ski resort weekends, singles ads, parents without partners groups, and other places, outlets, and events that women and men frequent to meet one another. You know these exist, and what you can or cannot feel comfortable with is a matter of personal fortitude and taste.

You also know that the most pleasant and promising ways to meet a pleasant and promising man are to get out of the house and accept invitations, ask an assortment of people to *your* place for an informal evening or weekend afternoon, find a job where there are lots of men, pursue your tennis or other interests when you can, do good works, and generally act with as much confidence and joie de vivre as you can manage. While you're doing all of this and while there's still no new love interest on the horizon, find a substitute man or men: look for a walker.

This might be an old pal—a man you are never going to fall in love with or have sex with but who is decent, interesting, and holds his own in a group.

He can be a social bonanza. You'll call him up when you need an escort for a fancy event. You'll invite him with a few of your old couple friends and some people from work to join you for a potluck meal, softball game, or whatever. Remember that you're setting up a new social structure and working on a long-term plan to include men—not necessarily *the* man—in your life. You don't want to spend *all* your time with women.

If you happen to know a walker, that's a break. If you don't, try to find one. He can't be married, for obvious reasons; he may be older than you, younger, gay, or straight.

Shortly after being dumped, one woman realized that her handiest social center, the place where she'd feel instantly familiar and comfortable, was the church she had attended sporadically for several years: "They have active and wide-ranging outreach programs, none of which I'd participated in before. I started volunteering for the Monday Hospitality Night, a meal in the church hall for about a hundred or so homeless each week, and on the Gay Men's Task Force. There I met two men who have become great friends. Knowing them and being able to invite one or the other has made it easier for me to get back into asking people over to my apartment for dinner. They're lively and intelligent, and they don't want to jump you at the first opportunity."

Sex, with and without a Man

One dumpee bemoans her enforced celibate state: "I always wondered how women had affairs with the proverbial milkman. Where can you find a milkman these days?"

In point of fact, chances are that the milkman or his equivalent is out there. You can have sex tonight, if you want to. Do you *really* want to?

Some women don't. Says Joy: "Sex didn't even cross my mind. In the beginning I was having enough trouble brushing my teeth and going to work. Just the thought of sex made me cringe. I got better, but now, three years later, I'm still not too concerned about sex. I feel this is a time for me to find out who I am. I'm still in the middle of going through something important.

"Here's where men and women are different, I think. A woman doesn't want to complicate her life by looking right away for somebody else. Men do that because they can't handle being on their own."

Some women *are* out there looking. From the sexually interested and active dumpees we've talked to, we can identify three kinds of behaviors—two to be avoided like the plague, one that may be fine.

They are:

- The mercy screw

In the immediate aftermath of being dumped, you may find one or two husbands of women friends or one of your business associates sniffing around your person. This is a fellow who sees you as a woman in need of a quick sex fix and himself as the man to help you out.

Says Allison: "A few weeks after my husband left, a man from his office, whom I had met at functions, called, and we talked for a long time. He called every day for a week, very solicitous, concerned about how I was doing, should he stop by, and so on. Finally I said he could come over. He brought a bottle of wine, I ended up crying on his shoulder, and we ended up in bed."

It was a mistake, she says. She didn't like him very much, she didn't feel in control of what she was doing, and he left with the air of a man who thought he had done a good deed and had a good lay at the same time.

Watch out for these guys. You can feel diminished *and* find yourself in various kinds of hot water. It may be difficult to disengage yourself from the man you slept with once and now hope never to see again.

- Mindless sex

One dumpee, desperate for a sexual connection, spent two or three years having a series of questionable relationships with young men during extended vacations in Central America: one was a man who sailed a boat (with her on it) up and down the coast and was twice stopped for drug inspections; closer to home, she got involved with a biker who spent most of his time on the road. Finally she came to her senses, realized she was damn lucky to have emerged from her wild days without a sexually transmitted disease or a police record, and now travels extensively with friends—another form of escape but at least a safer one.

If your craving for sex is so intense that you're tempted to get it on with any passing penis, remember these words from a seventy-two-year-old dumpee who has been on her own for the last twenty years: "Thank goodness we live in an electronic age. I've found vibrators and one or two other mechanical devices to be wonderful inventions. From time to time, I plan a special evening. I will have a glass of wine and a bubble bath, get out my bag of toys, have a great orgasm, and wake up in the morning refreshed—and with no back problems."

Says another woman: "I was at a party shortly after I was separated, and one of my dinner mates suggested that she and I walk instead of drive home—she had something important to tell me. We walked a while, chatted, me anticipating some advice about mutual funds or a possible job opening. Finally she said, 'Buy yourself a vibrator—soon.' It turned out to be a good suggestion."

• Friendly sex

Some women enjoy the possibility of sex with a man who won't become *the* man but who is kind, affectionate, fun, and won't leave her feeling depressed about herself in the morning.

Alice says: "A friend said to me, 'Sex isn't a big deal.' I don't agree. I know what it's like to have a regular and good sex life, and it *is* a big deal. It's a wonderful deal, and I don't want to forget it. If you know yourself, and you're not still deeply wounded, vulnerable, and liable to have sex for the wrong reasons with the first guy who presents himself—then go with your instincts, don't get hung up about it, and enjoy it."

Another woman says that two celibate years after she was dumped, she felt appealing and sexually attractive to men again: "One of the most hurtful fallouts of a breakup is that it makes you prickly or gives you a hard edge, and you have to overcome that unapproachable facade. When I was ready, I started to have fun. I did the male thing—having a lot of sex, even one-night stands. I was always careful—most men these days are, too, I find. I had never done this kind of thing before, and it was just playful and fun."

A woman who was married at twenty-one and separated at thirty-five says it was a couple of years before she could cope with "dating" again: "I certainly didn't have much experience in this department. I traveled a lot for business, and then I met a man from our home office. I began an affair with this terrific man that lasted, whenever we were in the same city, for over five years. I always thought sex was fun, but now it was delicious. Often we'd meet for lunch and then have 'dessert' in his hotel room or mine. This man did me a world of good. I stopped feeling and looking mournful. While geography and a lessening of his business travel mean that now we see each other only occasionally, we are still very good friends."

If your instincts are giving you the green light, proceed. If you can have fun and feel desirable and not see more than what's there, friendly sex might be a good idea.

But don't expect having sex again to be like riding a bicycle. If and when you do decide to go to bed with a man, the experience may be less than magical. It's not that you've forgotten *how*. It may simply take you a long time, longer than you would have thought, to feel relaxed, trustful, and sexually open. If you and Brad Pitt were stranded on a desert island, it would *still* take you a long time.

The Good News

When you start meeting and sizing up men and feeling ready for a new serious relationship in your life, you are definitely making progress. In fact, you may be surprised to note that you are often feeling even better than *before* the dumping.

Women we've talked to say:

- You're tougher.

"It's been a little scary to expose that vulnerability again to another man, to know that all the same hurts could arrive again," says Marion. "Because of that, I'm more guarded now than I used to be, more suspicious actually. I've got more radar now. If a man I was involved with but didn't know really well told me he was going away for a golf weekend with his brother, I'm not sure I'd believe him right off the bat. And I don't think this is a negative thing at all."

- Your expectations and your standards are higher.

"I was married so young and knew so little," says one woman, "that when the marriage was rocky, I kept quiet and left a lot unspoken. Now, with the man I'm seeing, I'm much more demanding of communication. I'm determined to deal with what's going on. I think that's a good thing that arises from all this—you have expectations now, you don't put up with crap the second time around."

- You know you can make it on your own.

Says one woman who has enjoyed an active social life for several postdumped years: "I don't deny that I'd like to settle down with a partner—someone to share my life with—since life is nicer that way. But here's what I see now as the ideal: he keeps his apartment, I keep my apartment, we're committed and faithful to each other, we do a lot of things together and a lot of things separately."

She thinks she will never give a hundred percent of herself to a man again but neither does she expect a hundred percent back: "Absolutely, you can trust again and have a wonderful love again. I've seen it happen with two close friends. But I think when you've been through what we've been through, you will always hold something of yourself in reserve, which is probably all to the good."

The Candidate

You have become involved with a potential love interest. Now you want to be really smart. Follow these five steps as you move through the early stages of a new relationship.

1) Try to learn how he has behaved with the previous women in his life.

If he has a history with women (as one hopes he does), the way he has treated them is the way he will treat you. You tend to think that *you* will be different, that whatever went on in his past has nothing to do with what will go on between the two of you. Assume you're wrong. Generally a man will repeat his former behavior, just as he'll go to the same restaurant over and over because he can't think of a new one. What he did to someone else to get to you is what he'll do to you to get to someone else. Men who dump live to dump again!

The exception to this truth is revealed in the Ben Bradlee/Hugh Hefner syndrome—a man with a lengthy history of bed partners who suddenly stops when he's sixtyish and the new woman is fifteen or more years younger. He figures this is as good as it's going to get, plus he's losing his taste for the chase. If you've connected with one of these guys, chances are he's yours for keeps.

If that's not the case, or even if it is, try to find out how his previous romances ended. Look for patterns. Come right out and *ask* him: "What have your past relationships been like? You were with Margaret for five years. She shared all that time with you, what would you think about inviting her over for drinks some evening with a few other people?" If he's smitten with you, he'll agree to what you want, even if he doesn't think it's such a sensational idea.

If what you learn about him is less than promising, it may not change your view—you may decide to forge ahead anyway—but at least you'll be armed with knowledge.

Says one woman: "When someone comes along in your life, you almost have to interview him. Expect honesty from him. You don't want to get stiffed again." And, she adds, be honest about yourself: "I've talked a little about my ex with the new men I've seen. Not in painful detail or to dwell on the past, but after fifteen years in my life and as the father of my two children, he's part of my story. And that makes it possible for the new man and me to compare experiences or to just understand each other better."

2) **Believe what he tells you about himself.**

When a man tells you something bad about himself, he's telling you the truth. So listen. Don't think, I'll change him, I'll make it different. Listen to his words, and take them as gospel because these warnings are the truth.

Says one woman: "The man I was with after my boyfriend left was fortunately honest enough to say, 'I can't make you promises. I'm not a faithful sort of guy. You'll want somebody else for the long term.' We had a good time together, and he and I parted as close friends."

3) **Negotiate your needs, or spell out what's acceptable and what's not, up front.**

Much has been made recently about couples' agreements, those written documents in which a man and woman who are thinking of joining forces list their individual intentions and expectations—everything from who pays what bills to how many times a week they'll have sex to where they'll go on vacation. While you may feel that's carrying things a bit far, you can and should let him know what's important to you.

Many dumpees look back and, seeing that they let their own needs slide in the relationship that is now over, determine not to do so again. Says one woman: "I realize now that I never made 'emotional draws' from my husband. I deferred things in my life, like running in the morning, because it made it less complicated for him. And so many times I didn't ask him to be there for me. Right after my mother died, he went on a camping trip. Although I was hurt, I didn't make a fuss. I won't do that kind of thing anymore. I've told the man I'm seeing now, 'Here are some things that matter to me, so respect them.'"

Jessica, with a busy job on a merchandising newsletter, remembers that on the two or three nights a month she really needed to work late her boyfriend invariably made plans for them or wanted to go out for the evening: "I'd pack up paperwork, go out with him, and then stay up until dawn getting my stuff done. I also felt responsible for making sure he wasn't bored on the few occasions when he had to wait for me. I'd keep newspaper or magazine clippings that I thought would interest him in my bag, and when I went to the ladies room in a restaurant, I'd give him these items to read so he'd be occupied while I was absent. It was absurd—and something I would never do again."

Jessica adds: "My mother often said, 'Never greet your husband at the door with bad news, and always have some food cooking so he knows dinner is under way.' I used to do that. Never bring up anything unpleasant before he had his drink and his dinner. We both worked all day, and in the evening I'd be running around, basically setting the stage for the King, and he'd be sitting unwinding with a scotch and the paper. A big mistake. One of my friends says, 'You should treat men mean to keep them keen.' Maybe there's something to that."

Deal openly with problems that arise, and demand that he face them too. If you and he need professional help, *insist* on it. Don't be afraid to challenge the man you're with for fear of causing conflict. Don't sweep things under the rug. Says one woman: "If I suspected he was veering off from the relationship, I wouldn't let thirty-six hours go by without dealing with the issue. I'll give him twenty-four hours, but after thirty-six, we're going to talk about it, and if talking about it together doesn't get anywhere, we're going to discuss it with a professional."

4) **If it's going nowhere, move on.**

Don't linger in a scene that clearly will not lead to the kind of relationship you want, whatever that is. Because you have been through the mill before, you will recognize signs and signals you can act on.

Says one woman: "I was dating a man who continued to see his supposedly former girlfriend. I let him know this was unsatisfactory to me, and I made a cutoff date in my mind past which I would not continue with him. He made no changes, the date came, and I said, 'OK, I'm not seeing you anymore.' He was suddenly hurt and upset and said he'd have nobody to talk to, because he and the other girlfriend evidently had nothing to talk about. I said, 'Then perhaps you should be thinking about who you want to be with, both horizontally *and* vertically.' He kept calling, and I never returned his calls."

That, of course, can be a powerful move. When a man thinks he can't have you anymore, that's when you become most valuable to him. The faster you become unavailable, the faster you'll get him back, if you want him. But *you must not be playing a game*—you must genuinely be moving on. And then, almost surely, you will discover you don't want him back, since the trust is not there.

5) If it ends, remember what you need to do to recover.

One woman says that when her marriage ended, she was a mess for a long time: "I woke up with panic attacks, shaking and feeling absolutely abandoned. When this new relationship ended, I 'processed' it. I let myself feel sad for a while, but I knew I had myself to depend on. I wasn't emotionally devastated. I knew *how* to get well, and I did. I knew it wouldn't defeat me."

You have the tools and the savvy to get yourself past the rocky stage and heal more quickly from an emotional upheaval.

• • •

The majority of women who contributed to *Dumped!* are admirably free of bile and bitterness. Says one: "Some men are great, some men aren't. I'm not down on men just because the one I loved walked away from me."

Being dumped has left you stronger and wiser. If you become involved with other men, you will never again put all your eggs in one basket. While you *may* be committed to someone new, you will always know that life holds its surprises. Nothing is an absolute. If you find a man, fine. If you don't, you can have a life for yourself that at the very least will be an honest one. And probably, if you play your cards right, it will be much, much more than that.

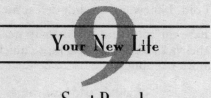

Your New Life

Sweet Rewards

You have exercised pain management and emerged intact from your walking wounded days, faced up to facing other people, reworked your attachment to your ex-man, repaired your damaged self-esteem, slogged out of the midway slump, and forged a new social order for yourself. Or maybe you're still working on some of these milestones.

In time you will be through the "dumped tunnel" and into the light. Then you should find, as many women have, that life can be good again.

If you are still not at this point, take heart and be encouraged by the women who share their experiences in this chapter. Individually, they have been past the great dump for stretches of time ranging from three to twenty-five years. Some are contentedly single; some are remarried or in new, happily committed relationships. Some regret that there is no new man with whom to share their lives. All have found satisfactions they would never have imagined possible at the start.

I Relish the Simple Pleasures

"Of course," says Donna, "the best thing, the *delicious* thing about living without a man is simply that I can do whatever I want, whenever I want. When I need to take care of myself or family or friends, I can, without having to worry about what this man wants."

Other women talk similarly about the simple pleasures they now enjoy:

> "I can water my garden early in the morning. Previously, in order not to wake up my husband, I had to do my watering at night, which gave my roses black spot. Now I water in the day, and my roses and I are both happier."

> "I don't have to share a bathroom! Those whiskers in the sink drove me crazy."

> "I turn on the light in the middle of the night if I want to read. And I lie in my own bed and read instead of having to go out to the living room so I won't wake him up. I don't have to tiptoe around anymore."

> "Sometimes I give myself a whole day off just to veg out, and I never feel guilty. Occasionally I feel lonely, but I have so many

options when that hits: friends are supportive, and one of them is always available to see a movie, talk on the phone, or take a walk."

"I covered up for him in little ways. When he made a joke at the dinner table and the kids didn't laugh, I'd say something that meant, 'Oh, isn't Dad funny.' I don't have to do that now. My new life with my children is very simple and healthier."

"I don't cook meat anymore—ever. What a pleasure!"

I Love the Freedom

Says Victoria: "Living solo is liberating, spontaneous, self-centered, decadent. I now do what pleases me. What I eat, how I entertain, who my friends are—it's all my decision.

"I give a lot in a relationship, I think we all do, and I realize now that with Brent I accommodated and compromised all the time. Being on your own brings with it a terrific sense of freedom. Once you learn to live with yourself and like yourself, spending time alone is heavenly. I never get enough!"

Says another dumpee: "The other day my girlfriend, also unattached, said, 'Ah, freedom!' And I said, 'Isn't it absolutely phenomenal?' I don't know where I'll be or what I'll be doing five years from now. I find that exciting!"

I Can Remember the Good Times with Pleasure

Say what you will, according to many women, 'twas better to have been dumped than never to have been loved.

Lynn, whose husband informed her in a phone call that he wouldn't be coming home from his business trip for Christmas, or indeed ever again, found herself angrily thinking for a long time, I've given him a huge chunk of my life. Then gradually, she says, that attitude started to feel wrong and misguided: "Nothing that was good should be considered a waste."

Sheila for a long time felt tearful and blue when she remembered a great experience she had shared with her ex-boyfriend. Now, she says, she can recall those times with pleasure: "Recently I passed a spa that Mario and I had gone to once for 'A Day of Beauty.' He had decided on a lark to come with me, and he had a facial, manicure, massage—the works, all this stuff he would never do. We both felt so goofy and silly, I remember laughing the whole time. I think about that day now, and it makes me smile."

After the pain and anger have died down, many women regain a comforting perspective on the relationship that ended. Says one: "I'm so glad I had that marriage and have my children. I would never have given that up, even if I had to go through three times the pain I experienced after John left.

"I think I finally felt I was going to be OK, really OK, when I realized that my marriage represented a quarter of a century of my life. It will always be a part of who I am—part of my history, part of my personal drama. And that's OK. It was good *once*, and I feel happy about that."

My Friendships Are Deeply Rewarding

Many women say they felt constrained while in the relationship and socialized mostly with people the ex-man wanted to see. And now they don't have to. "I love getting together with friends," says one woman, "without worrying about what he thinks of them."

They find themselves drawing even closer to those women who have been with them through thick and thin. "I used to cancel a plan with a woman friend to do something with a partner," says Barbara. "Now it's the other way around. Even though I have several men friends I adore, I value my female friends more. They are constants."

Some women learned the folly of investing all their emotional energies in husband and family. Rhona, now remarried, is determined not to repeat that mistake: "There is no question that I will never again allow myself to become so wrapped up in husband and kids that I don't make the effort to become close to other people as well. I think my first husband did the same thing, actually—he too isolated himself. I believe the affairs he had, that ultimately crumbled the marriage, were attempts to get away from that isolation.

"I've made some good friends in recent years, and in my new marriage I'm keeping some turf for myself. Men have always done this. They have their poker night or golf Sunday or whatever."

Nothing Fazes Me Now

Women come out of being dumped with a new sense of empowerment. Says Darcy: "When you are deeply committed to a relationship that is, against your wishes and to your dismay, pulled out from under you, the worst thing you can imagine happening has actually *happened*. Once you press on and get through it, you feel you can handle anything that comes at you for the rest of your life."

Beverly says: "My dad died when he was fifty, so my mom was on her own. My big fear, I see now, was that Martin, my husband, would die and leave me on my own. And in a way, for me, he did die. My greatest fear came to pass. So what's left to fear?"

Laura expresses the same thought when she talks about an adventure she had two years after being dumped: "I trekked in Nepal for thirty days, with four men, at very high altitudes. It was the best thing I could have done. I was not at all afraid, because my worst fear had already happened. I haven't looked back, and now I'm not afraid of anything."

I'm Managing My Money

Many women enjoy the fact that whatever money they have is theirs. A few divorced dumpees have found that their financial state, if not lavishly comfortable, is at least less volatile than before, when their ex-men were leading their double lives.

Says Paula, co-owner of a popular gift shop: "I have always worked and made a good income. And yet in my first marriage, I basically turned everything over to my husband. He was a stockbroker, and I thought he could handle money better than I could. In fact, I can manage money very well. I just got lazy about it, and I thought I *should* let him take control.

"One of the real pluses gained from the whole miserable time is that I've achieved some street smarts about finances. Although I've remarried, I'm protecting myself in various ways. It doesn't have to be done in an intrusive or hostile manner, and it actually makes for a healthier relationship. Men do it, and it doesn't negate the intimacies of the marriage."

I Spend More Time Now Doing Something Good for Others, and That Feels Good for Me

As they have sought to build lives that include new friends and are not partner-centered, many dumpees have become involved in reaching out to people who can use their help.

Janet acknowledges that the initial impetus to do good works was a self-serving one. She was eager to meet people who had never seen or heard of or had anything to do with her ex-man: "I started volunteering at a shelter, and from that I got caught up in the concerns of homeless people. I have a fair amount of clout in this city and some useful connections, and I decided to put that to work. Over the past two years I've been instrumental in raising close to a million dollars from private donations to help fund housing for homeless women. That I've been able to do something good for somebody else has reenergized my spirit."

Jean, seventy-eight and contentedly on her own for many years, has little patience when a friend complains of feeling lonely: "Stop thinking about how you feel—start thinking about how you can help someone who's in a lot worse shape than you are. And those people are all around you."

I'm a Kinder, Gentler Person

Says Deidre, an attorney: "In the old days, I felt pretty invincible. I couldn't have had a better life, I would have said, on every level. And I think that made me hard on other people. When I saw female clients who were sobbing about one thing or another, in the back of my mind was the thought, Well, just pull up your socks and get on with it. I can run my life, why can't you do the same?

"Getting dumped was a dose of reality, and it's made me more compassionate. There was nothing so precious and special about me after all. I'm vulnerable, too. I'm now not only a better person but a better lawyer."

Suzanne was surprised and moved by the responses of a few friends and even casual acquaintances who, when she was first on her own, called to offer kind thoughts or stopped by with a little food and good cheer: "I suddenly realized how important and helpful those gestures were. And I also realized it was the sort of thing I had never done for others. My life was my work and my family. While I was always effective at getting the after-school program extended from grade three to grade seven, that sort of thing, I was definitely not the mother who would be there with the hot dogs on field day. Never the kind of woman who'd think of taking cookies over to a sick or lonely neighbor to make her feel better. I do that now."

I've Got a Whole New Career

Says Emilie: "After Harris ended our five-year relationship, I wanted a whole fresh start. I left nursing, and now I'm working for a brokerage house. After never having done office work before, here I am with two computers on my desk. It's a high-energy place, and I'm absolutely loving it, learning and growing all the time."

Another dumpee, who needed to find a job fast, nervously accepted a secretarial position with an executive search firm. Today she's in great shape: "I've learned to love change! Now I go after opportunities, and I never say no to a new job. Once I gained some confidence and learned new skills, I started applying for developmental opportunities at work, and now I have a rich, varied trail of work experience. I've also discovered what kind of work I love to do, through a process of elimination and growth."

My Kids and I Are Very Close

Susan's children were ten and thirteen at the time her husband left, and they weekended and vacationed with their father. Those were often difficult times, says Susan, but now her young-adult children are among her best friends: "It's enormously satisfying to know my kids respect me. Even though being dumped was emotional hell, and they saw the pain I went through, both have told me they always felt I was there for them no matter what."

Marriage?
Been There, Done That

"When I was at the height of my misery in the early days after my husband left, two or three women indicated that they were sort of envious of me," says Louisa, on her own for fourteen years. "And I would think, Are you out of your mind? But later what that said to me was, many people are unhappy in their marriages. They are afraid to leave or don't have the wherewithal to leave. And that's really sad.

"I still believe in marriage and family, but my life has changed so much. I doubt I'd have the patience to be married again. I've done it. I feel no anxiety whatsoever about being unmarried."

I'm My Own Person Now

Women talk about postdumped survival as a time of peeling away the layers of the onion, getting to the core of themselves. They are pleased and at peace with what they now see before them.

"I come from a really wonderful family," says one woman. "I have great parents and a great brother, and lately my sense has been, I'm back home, I'm myself again. I feel I know myself quite well and am happier with who I am than ever before."

I'm Grateful for My Life

"You know," says Joan, "I just have to think of myself as a fortunate person. I have a lovely home—hardly a mansion, but I've pruned the trees and the wisteria and the hedge for the past twenty-five summers. I have friends, good food, good memories, books, music.

"Sometimes I tell a younger friend, 'Use your good fortune. It's time to be creative. It's time to be us. We do not have to please everyone else. Don't waste any of that time. It's gone before you know it.'"

Afterword

I remember very well the first time I ever heard the word *dumped* in a context that had nothing to do with removing trash. It was an early fall afternoon in 1958, and I came home from school in Philadelphia to find my mother and two of her friends sitting in the living room talking about "that sweet Debbie Reynolds" who had been dumped by Philadelphia's own Eddie Fisher, who had run off with Elizabeth Taylor. They all agreed it was just terrible. How could Eddie have done this to that nice girl and those dear little children? It was clear then who was the wronged party, and the conclusion was that Eddie had done something that should make him feel very, very guilty.

Jump to this era, when very few of us want to be judgmental and many view all lives as "works in progress." When a woman gets dumped these days, her immediate circle will certainly gather round, but as we've said, most people don't want to become enmeshed in taking sides.

The main point I hope you will remember is that *you* have to heal yourself, although you can certainly get help. The passage of time will eventually form some nice scar tissue. Life *will* go on.

Accept that there is nothing you can do about what has happened—you have been well and truly dumped. It is difficult to acknowledge that you have no control over something that drastically alters the direction of your life. Do not obsess about this.

While working on this book, I had an experience that seemed to bring me full circle. I went to hear a talk by Debbie Reynolds as part of a program called "Unique Lives." She was terrific in describing her life and its ups and downs. She spoke briefly about Eddie Fisher's departure and of her second husband, who managed to lose all the money she had earned over the years. Her third husband, she said, was a southern gentleman, and for a while it looked as if all would be well. Then one day she heard him saying over and over, "I miss Virginia." She thought he meant the state. He didn't. He meant a Ms. Virginia—and then he too was gone.

Three husbands, she said, were enough, and she was out of that game—but who knows? She's famous for playing someone who was unsinkable. And she added: "Either you give up or you go on."

That's it! Most of us think that you only go around once. So it's up to each of us to never give up and to go on to build a productive life.

If all goes well (and it will), one day you'll find that you think back with pleasure on the good times you *did* have with that man who later dumped you. And a wonderful haze will have descended over the bad times.

It helps, of course, if a new man comes into your life, but even if one doesn't, remember that you are a person who has been tested in a very nasty way and you have survived. A number of women I met express a view very like my own: "I was better prepared mentally for the possibility of a fatal illness than I was for being dumped. I will never be so stupid again. Whatever happens, I'm living an honest life—no more accepting less than I deserve and never again accepting a diminishing role in the life of a man I love."

While it may sound odd to you now if your wound is raw, believe me when I say that some women I talked to think that getting dumped was the best thing that ever happened to them. One woman told me that she has actually thought of writing a thank-you note to her former husband. Her feeling is that being dumped forced her to take a good second look at her life and what she wanted. She took her time and concentrated on her career and her young son. Now, five years later, she is remarried to a man who gives her the kind of companionship and support that she had previously only dreamed about. Her teenage son gave the toast at her second wedding and remarked that now *everyone* was happier. It *can* happen.

The vast majority of the women who shared their experiences with me have emerged into rewarding lives. They have expanded their horizons and learned to truly like themselves. I was amazed at the number who have tested themselves by going trekking in Nepal, even a few who look as if a ski hill in Vermont would be a more suitable challenge. It's surprising what going back to square one can do for you.

As Debbie Reynolds said: "Either you give up or you go on." The first is not an option for any of us.

Now that you have read *Dumped!*, do you have any thoughts or experiences you would like to share?

If so, please write to:

Sally Warren
P.O. Box 4858
Blaine, WA 98231-4858